Just Three Lads

By

Roy Thersby

Just Three Lads

First Published, 2014
Second Published, 2022

The Thersby Group

77 Norton Road

Stockton on Tees

TS18 2DA © Thersby Group 2022.

Reworked for Amazon paperback and Kindle digital media May 2022

Some of the characters in this book are fictitious, as are the situations and dealings carried out.

I hope you enjoy reading my presentation, I had many hours of enjoyment writing and the creation of the situations described within this novel.

Just Three Lads

People in the book

Terry or Tel, The eldest brother, and teller of the tale.

Leslie or Les, The middle brother.

Kevin or Kev, the youngest brother.

Nobby, the garage mechanic and driver.

Suzy, a very nice lady.

Lizzy, Suzy's not so nice twin sister

Clarissa Suzy's sister-in-law

Fanny, the proprietor of Syd's café.

Geordie, a guy from the race track.

Katy, busty wife of Geordie

Jimmy, deceased husband of Suzy.

The two girl's daughters of Jimmy and Suzy.

Charles, the nice lawyer.

DS Harper, Stolen vehicle squad officer.

Ian, the jovial farmer.

Just Three Lads

Mr Sangster, First rate nasty Dude.

Mr Twiddle Dum. Henchmen number 1

Mr Twiddle Dee. Henchmen number 2

Mr John Wade, the other garage owner.

Forward

The *Time Gentleman bell* rang out in the bar, the old man sank the last dregs from his glass of beer, wished good night to his favourite barmaid then proceeded to wobble home. Finding his way was as natural as an inward bound homing pigeon, regardless of his state he knew how to open the door so quietly let himself in, make it to his favourite arm chair then fall asleep, sometimes the rest of the house didn't know he was home.

However, this evening he followed the railing along towards the entrance to his old Victorian terrace house, we presume he stumbled put his arm out to steady himself on the railings, missed his hold then fell down the steps to the one-time servant's entrance in the basement, landing in a heap by the front door.

The autumn weather took a turn for the worse that evening, with him still outside the house in a crumpled position the finger of fate was not on his side.

The solicitor reading out his last Will and testament most of the inheritance went to the latest of the family, some monies were destined to a part of the family, I had not heard of.

Then there was a named family that nobody knew off but he had left provision in his will, we found out later it was a family he had with his favourite bartender, now we know why he drank at that bar, we did not like the beer, so we supported another bar.

The Solicitor managing the reading was too much of a gentle man to read out what he had written for any other parties laying claim to his estate, telling them in advance, where they could put their claim.

I must admit that the room rocked with laughing when that part became common knowledge. Together with an accidental death payment there was an extra amount of money payable to the family this consisted a few thousands, this was divided equally between the current family members.

Kevin, Leslie, and Terry, we were to receive the business with Terry being the eldest was to have the final say in any decision.

A codicil was announced then read out after the solicitor had declared the business transfer to the three lads was any family members not happy with the terms of the will were to be cut out, their share was then to be divided equally between the other family members. That caused a few quiet mutterings, but nobody spoke up.

I thought to myself that finally we get to run this business the way we wanted without the interference that the old man caused.

Chapter 1

I am Jim, I have been driving so far for an hour heading for the Hull ferry terminal to catch the overnight ferry to Rotterdam.

My companion on this trip was the latest addition to the company, a likeable woman called Elizabeth, I reckon she was around thirty; she presented herself very well and had an impeccable dress sense which complimented her blonde hair.

After a week or so I realised that she was a career and social climber, she would advance herself in anyway available to her, these women seem to be attracted to the good times, the bad times, desirable situations, slippery as a snake and probably more dangerous.

The vehicle we were driving for this trip was an excellent well-equipped motorhome. Although a bit over the top for boxes of paperwork it was the idea of one of the partners, he probably had plans for it in the future. A company of large international accountants employed me, and my work within the company was a logistic basis to move security documents, sealed pouches; from one company department to another. We also moved other stuff. In all cases the contents of the pouches and packages were unknown to us. We used to use a security courier but an increase in their charges lost them the contract, the boss decided to trial this form of transportation for a period, then see how the costs balanced out.

Just Three Lads

This trip I had intended doing a bit of business for myself, I wasn't that excited driving from A, to B.

I was an unemployed precision engineer. I had read in the International Engineer publication a small Belgium Aerospace company had recently been put up for sale, the owner had died.

They didn't have a successor; nobody was interested to take over the business. It was a chance, I would like to take on, to make a start into a market, that I believed is always looking for good engineers, also my family could make a new start, a new town, a different culture, a new challenge.

As we were driving Elizabeth was mooching around in the motorhome checking stuff opening draws looking in the cupboards.

Without me knowing, she had picked up my briefcase flipped open the lid, then remarked have you won the lottery?

I didn't know what she meant, and looked at her sitting on the passenger seat with the briefcase open on her lap. Hey if you don't mind, that's my briefcase what is in it is private, that is all my paperwork leave it alone!

She must have seen, or flicked open an envelope, in which I had put money for which I would use as deposit for the new business.

I wish, I replied, a lottery win would change everything; I went on to say that, the money was our savings to be used as a deposit for a future to secure a better life for my family.

Then she replied. Are you sure this has not been skimmed from the cash we carry on these trips abroad?

My gut reaction was "You cheeky cow."

I replied What cash! I have not seen any money in what we carry. It is all office documents from the Head office to the Belgian Company in Brussels. She went on about this for a while and was really getting on my nerves; I told her to shut up and be quiet, the problem, if there was such a problem, would be sorted out, when we got home and I would bring the matter up at head office.

It was prearranged that the Belgian office staff removed the parcels, and the paperwork the van was taken by the Garage serviced, refuelled, and made ready for the return trip.

Natalie, my favourite receptionist, she ran the Belgian office, saw me, she gave me the customary, cheek to cheek greetings.

She proceeded to accept all our packages, and rolled her eyes as she looked at me.

Problem?

No, just I have lots of paperwork to start after you have gone. She passed over to me, a large envelope to take back with me for the Head office, wished me a Bon Voyage home.

Then she whispered who is the lady with you, is it your lover?

No, I whispered she just joined the company and came with me to experience the trip.

Has she had much experience asked with a flutter of her eyelids, I knew exactly what she meant, I replied how would I know that?

You are man she replied.

The outer door to the office opened, in walked the maintenance guy, at the reception desk, he dropped the keys for the RV, claiming it is already. He continued speaking, to Natalie in her native tongue,

Natalie translated for me what the man had said, He had stored some documentation for Head office in the back of the vehicle.

Leaving Brussels, we headed south towards a small village where the Aerospace company I was interested in is based.

When we arrived, the outside of the building was not impressive, remnants of a post war start up unit, but let me see what was inside before I decided.

I left Lizzy sitting in the RV and went to view, after a quick walk round, it was obvious some of the choice machines had already gone, probably, the machinery had been leased, and the leasing company had recovered them.

For what I saw and they brief explanation the family were not going to sell the land, they intended to rent it. At that point I decided that it was not for me. Lizzy had made herself a coffee, as I appeared she offered to make me a cup, she had taken a stroll found a patisserie, acquired some very tasty looking pastries, that shop would have been the only bonus, if I had moved over here to commence work.

Just Three Lads

Heading for the ferry, luck had it, we drove straight onboard, Elizabeth again watching all and sundry looking for her perfect man in the Bar then returning to her cabin.

I was up early, this Ferry depending on tides docking varied to certain times, but dismemberment was always listed as at nine a.m. I took the chance to eat a quick breakfast, then as we drove out of the ferry terminal, I observed the men from the custom having good look at our vehicle, I thought any moment we would get the signal to pull over, but we got a wave through.

After clearing Custom's, we headed towards the motorway M18 West bound, then I would take the A1M North.

I observed on the horizon black storm clouds, with the distinct shadow of heavy rain falling from underneath the cloud bank, I knew that as we hit the A1M the land to the east was high moorland, as rain clouds are forced higher, they tend to dump the water on anything underneath, that cloud bank was about to cut across our path.

I remarked that if that rain is bad, we could pull over have a coffee and one of those pastries and let the storm pass us by.

Lizzy thought that a good idea, she went into the back of the van, and started to prepare some food and hot drinks, then a large car over took me and cut in front,

I swerved to avoid him, as I evaded the pending accident, a shout from behind me, Lizzy was hanging on to a side cupboard.

I flashed my headlights he flashed its hazard warning lights twice, as he sped off.

Was that a weak offering of an apology for bad driving or what?

Did you see that large car, he slowed down, swerved in front of me, then flashed its hazard lights, then he buggered off; what a Berk I thought?

Elizabeth said yes, I spilt some food down my blouse as you swerved to avoid him

Just then the approaching storm unleashed its might, it was as if we had driven into a water fall, the wipers were having a hard time shifting the torrents of rain water on the wind screen, I was having difficulties viewing the road ahead, remarking now is the time to park up, and let this storm clear.

I could just see a sign reflecting in my headlights, a movement in the rear-view mirror, distracted my attention from the road ahead to Elizabeth was standing behind me, and was removing her blouse.

I did not let her know, that I had seen her do this, I was enjoying the striptease.

I reduced my speed further, as we continued up the road. My view in the mirror was good enough for the time being, but trying to keep an eye on the road and a swinging pair of tits at the same time, was getting to be a problem. My imagination was running wild, I thought about what it would be like with a full unrestricted view.

Just Three Lads

She slipped off her bra, her breasts were nicely matched; I thought she was going to continue with the striptease but she began to put on another blouse. She returned to the front cabin, and sitting beside me showing off her legs in her new high heeled shoes.
"They are nice shoes"
"Yes, they are, thank you."

I was turning into the lay by; another vehicle was also turning in, I slowed to follow him.
She remarked I have a desire,
oh yes, I replied,
I always wanted to have sex in a thunderstorm, I want to have sex with you in this lay-by.
I have never been propositioned before, it was a tempting offer, we were on our own, who would know.
Before I could answer, she was starting playing with the buttons on her blouse. She was becoming a distraction." I replied "let me stop in this lay-by."
"Ok" she replied.
As I turned into the lay-by, she blew me a kiss. The wagon in front, had slowed as he eyed up the first available parking space, but decided to move further up the lay-by leaving me the first space.

I could easily park behind the large truck, there was enough room, although difficult to see with the rain now bouncing back up from the road a couple of feet, but in a minute, Lizzy might get what she desired.

Just Three Lads

I turned my head totally distracted, then I was about to stop, Elizabeth had her blouse undone to the waist She was flashing her breasts.
She was going to have sex in a thunderstorm, and it was going to happen, this very day.

I did not see the large section of girder extending over the wagons flat body, his warning sign was swinging freely and must have been edge on to my vision, the girder punched out the driver's screen, the airbag inflated, and doing it designed action, covered my face; the momentum of the motorhome still rolled forward, I was impaled on the end of that fucking girder, the driver's seat back broke off, leaving me and seat laid out. The van stopped moving as the vehicle impacted together. The bumpers had done their job, all but this stupid lump of girder stuck firmly in my face.

I felt a jolt, felt also heard a thud, my nose experienced a sickening stench and a snotty smell.
Then nothing; blackness silence, a ring of bright lights seemed to dance Infront of me.
I realised I was hurt, my senses were slowly returning, I tried to sit up, but this steel girder kept me pinned to the seat, the darkness of the thunderstorm was waning, second by second, a strange blue light had surrounded me, everything I looked at was surrounded in this blue light.

Just Three Lads

Then something seemed to touch my hand, I looked to see, a hand in the darkness, holding my fingers, a soft female voice whispered "Come with me Jim."
It was a voice I knew but where from?
Then my view changed, I was outside the vehicle.

Although blurred, I could make out Elizabeth was still laid out in the passenger seat, unsteadily she stood, she looked, vile obscenities flowing from her mouth, she was cursing aloud, Lizzy also taking stock of her situation, quickly realised, what had happened.

Now standing, she carefully shook the broken pieces of glass from her clothing, and other nasty items crashes seem to generate, the remnants now littered the inside of the motorhome cabin area.
She had blood on her shoulder,
I called out, "There is a first aid box under the passenger seat."
she took no notice.
Slowly extracting her handbag from the mess, she opened the door and stepped down away from the carnage that was once a luxury motorhome.
Calmly shook her clothes again to make sure no glass particles were clinging to her clothing, tapping her shoes on the side of the van to dislodge any further objects, she looked round for someone to help.
There was nobody.
She re-entered the van, retrieved her coat, then spying me laid on the driver's seat carefully extracted my briefcase from beside me.

Just Three Lads

Flipping open the briefcase she inspected the contents.
"Thank you, Jim, I will accept this as severance pay,
as I do not think we will be working again together."
She was taking my money the money I had saved for
buying the new business.
I shouted to her give that to Suzy it is hers, she took no
notice, I felt shocked with the pure cold-hearted action
of that bitch, and a so-called work colleague.

Then the voice in my head saying,
"Don't bother, she is not within our ambience,"
I looked around to see where the voice was coming
from, the voice was in my head.

I looked around, there was a vision of my mother-in-
law, she was smiling back at me.
Now, she never ever smiled at me, something was
wrong, together with the fact, also she was killed six
months earlier in a skiing accident in Norway.
She was skiing; slipped off a downhill slope, hit a
boulder unfortunately covered by snow.
It was the freakiest accident as another meter and she
would have cleared the obstacle, but it still claimed a
life, of a lovely woman taken before her time.

Sonja whispered, "We have things to do, and places to
go, come.
however, you are here, what has happened? a million
questions, already forming in my brain.
Then I saw, Elizabeth starting to leave the van. "Wait I
said what is Elizabeth doing"?

Elizabeth with my briefcase in hand, and a hand towel in the other, stopped, looked back inside, blew a kiss towards the body left in the motorhome then closed the door.

I was shocked by what she was doing the way she was acting, the heartless Cow.

The rain had stopped, she walked up the lay-by, covering her head with the towel as she walked under a tree still dripping rain water, passed the parked-up wagon, no sign of the wagon driver.

Then saw a parked car with a couple inside, she asked the driver could they take her to a police station, she had just been in an accident.

She climbed into the car just as the door closed, she mumbled to herself, well that was an expected bonus and disappointment, the car left taking her to safety.

Chapter 2

Twenty months later,

We finally had taken over the old man's business.

We had worked out our cash flow, it was a strange feeling to sit and plan the future between the brothers, I was surprised in the suggestion that came from the other two guys, then we agreed to agree and decided to dispense with the breaking of vehicles for spare parts.
Another decision we made was to concentrate on the salvage and recovery side, although sometimes messy it was a good earner and made money.

The clearing out of the main yard was interesting, the income from the spares increased, I reckon it was down to common knowledge the stock was on clearance or it went for scrap.
We also hit it lucky the value of scrap went to an all-time high; we really made a large profit.

The land was cleared, we had plans professionally drawn up, then decided amongst us to the new layout of the yard.

We had a new concrete hard standing laid, as we found a cement company that was extremely willing to dump partly set concrete for free, all we had to do was to make sure we had a tractor setup and ready to level the stuff as it landed.

Just Three Lads

In the end we had a reasonably good hard standing area to work with, we added a couple of buildings and larger sheds, to keep the taller vehicles in.

The living quarters for the brothers were next to each we each had a view of the yard from our living room within the flat, and a view of the sea from our bedrooms.

The garage layout looked good from my window; I was the closest to the office and main gate, the office was to the right of the main gate and entrance from the outside street. The large work sheds were opposite, the compound as well as safe storage to my right,

We had liked the idea of living on the premises, and as we owned the land; it put a stop to the burglars from breaking in and stealing stored and crashed vehicles.

In away none of us had a long way to travel when we got a call out to recover from accident sites.

We had built our fortress, it was up to us, to police it, and make it work.

In a garage not far from madness by the sea, a radio was playing rock music, laughter, with cries of a jovial nature, awoke me from my sleep, these noises were coming from the main garage.

I listened for a while, then I tried to continue with my sleep, alas I had I am not sure how to explain the feeling, it was a nagging feeling, something wasn't right made me get up and look from the window.

Although I had a good view of the yard, all seemed quiet but the main door to the garage was open, I dressed and walked into the garage, I saw a car on the car lift, all the wheels removed, the back axel and rear suspension laid on a hydraulic workbench under the rear of the car.

My brother Les was sitting on a garage seat examining the suspension components.

"What's happened to that?

Les lifting his head, "Hi Terry I am not sure, it came in with the rear axle locked solid but I cannot find the problem.

" Kevin took off the wheels and then dropped the axle but it is all free.

"Where is Kevin Now?"

"He went to the bog with a stomach ache."

"Why did he take all this apart"?

"He was hoping to fix it quick for the ladies",

"Where are the ladies"?

"Oh, they are waiting for the car to be repaired; they are in the waiting room."

"What have you found is it the engine or gearbox"?

"The engine runs, the gearbox changes gear."

Walking under the car the main driveshaft was hanging from the gearbox, a bright mark of polished steel caught my attention, taking a closer look,

I saw the problem, the driveshaft flexy joint had peeled open, I pulled it clear of the gearbox.

I tried to turned it back and fro, the swivel joint had locked solid.

Hey les, "This is the part that broke up and jammed the transmission." Kevin's enthusiasm had made the repair into a £500 job instead of a ton.

How do we cost this job without making a loss?

"What are the owners like"?

"They seem to be down to their last pennies, a couple of girls with their mum."

Just Three Lads

Well, I thought let us see what can be done, saying to Les "Go and put the kettle on and make the customers some coffee, I will be back in a few minutes, going to get changed"

Thinking on the run, I thought let us get it back together then help the poor souls out.

Returning to the job, I studied the problem this flexy joint had caused. Now the bad news, it wasn't what we normally carried in our stock.

But I thought there may be a way, it was Sunday, no suppliers open, we didn't have one of these cars or a second-hand unit in stock.

Tomorrow was a Bank holiday so all supplies were closed again, so for two days, we may be lumbered with unwanted guests.

Les came back with a coffee for me, saying he would have his shift finished by 8:30, then he would have to go and get some kip.

I sent Kevin my youngest bro to wash the big wrecker truck, that would keep him busy for a while.

I quickly worked my magic on rebuilding the suspension and had it all back together in 20 minutes.

I now was missing a few bolts and the faulty swivel joint. I grabbed a sweeping brush, and swept the floor around the area under the car, and found the parts.

The flexi swivel joint was a three-swivel version we had four swivel ones, unfortunately they will not fit.

A voice from the shadows said. "Hello you",

Now that was a voice, I had known from the past.

I turned to greet the person I remembered with the voice, a pleasant surprise the girl I remembered was now the woman. She had married flown the nest, and I had lost contact, she looked as lovely as I remembered.

Who could forget the most piercing green eyes I have ever seen, shoulder length sandy coloured hair, she was dressed, in a dark blue loose sweater, blue jeans and boots.

She was enquiring what the problem with the car was, I explained that the swivel joint had seized then split open that was the cause of the problem.

She then asked why the back end of the car dismantled for that little repair was.

This woman is not stupid, and she had sussed that there was a problem.

So, honesty being the best policy, I explained about Kevin's enthusiasm in dismantling cars, and not getting it correct.

She thanked me for my answer, then said would I be able to repair the joint?

Replying, I would if I had one, and as we talked, I kept on re-assembling the vehicle.

I was thinking on my feet, the problem, the joint was unique to that make of car.

Suzy enquired "Do I have a problem"?

"It would seem so, unless I find a joint, or work out where I can get one from, this car is staying put."

She replied "Oh Dear, now your problem has created a new problem for me, she went on to explain, I have a meeting in the city on Tuesday, also the car was her only means of transport. Her funds were already running low, with the cost of the repair could be devastating.

She asked would it be possible that she leave the car with us and return when she could?"

"That for me personally would not be a problem, but I am only part owner of the business.

The rules of the garage and storage it would be expensive, after a week or so and the car was not of great value", she did agree with my situation.

I will try and sort this matter out to our mutual satisfaction."

Where was the meeting to take place"?

She replied, "It was at a solicitor's office in the city fifty miles south from here."

Her destination was near to a racing circuit, I would have liked to go too, I would have watched it on the TV, but really, I was only looking for any excuse to go and watch it live.

Meet up with a couple of chums, as well as get the updated gossip from within the trade.

Chapter 3

A solution flashed through my mind, maybe I could take Suzy and her daughters with me.

I could watch the bike races, meet up with my friends, take her to her business meeting.

But that would only happen if she was willing, we would return on the Tuesday, obtain a flexi joint. Then I could fix the car, she and her family would be on their way and a hopefully we could keep in touch in the future.

What could go wrong?

I must admit, I did have a soft spot for her.

Bouncing this revised idea off her, it was the best option to her situation.

Or maybe; we could travel up later today, camp overnight, watch the bike racing, then I drop you at your meeting Tuesday, and whilst she was in her meeting, I could get the new part for her car, then pick you after your meeting, drive back here, fix the car, then she would be on her way.

"Aha she replied, a problem, sleeping in the car, all in one car may cause a problem, and she wasn't really happy with camping."

Yes, I could see her point, If I was driving a car, but would it be a problem if I was driving that." I pointed to a sleek looking motorhome, parked in the corner of the yard.

It came my way a few years ago.

Just Three Lads

It recovered from an accident, the customer never returned for it, we did try to contact him, and over the years, then we claimed it for the accrued storage charges."

I passed the keys to her, go look and see if it will suit you for this weekend.
Ok, Suzy gave me a lovely smile and walked off towards the motorhome.
While I was in the office, I checked for the part on the computer, two parts suppliers were listing them around £50.00. Then I thought what if, I checked out the internet used spares page, luck had it I found a complete second hand one listed, it was reduced to £5.00.
Suzy came back looking a lot happier in herself.
She was happy with the motorhome, that rear bedroom would be able to keep the noise from the girls away from me, I laughed you mean keep the smelly mechanic away from the kids.
I will have you know; I have been known to scrub up well in certain cases.

She offered that they would give the motorhome or the recreational vehicle (RV) a clean and spruce up, making it presentable for the trip.
I gave her a sideways look; would I need the dinner jacket and black tie for the weekend?
She looked back at me with the stare; only women can do, and said not this weekend, just a good scrub will do, then fell into fits of laughter.

Ok it was a deal. I accepted her offer, suggesting she could use it whilst here.

I would come over and connect the van to the main electricity supply and fresh water, so they could clean and do what women do when they are in housekeeping mode.

I also mentioned the parts I had found, her smile slipped when I said the cost of the new parts, but beamed again when I said, we would be picking up a second-hand part at the racetrack, it was only £5.00.

Wow, a fiver, how and where did I find one

I mentioned locating one on the fleabay internet auction,

I found this local chap selling one. I gave him a call, and it works out he is going to the bike races as well, I said we will take the old one and compare them when we meet, but even if they are different, the swivel joint may be the correct size, then I can work magic and make the original serviceable again.

Suzy smirked; Magic, Wahey; I replied with my best Tommy cooper impression "A, HA, Yes Just like that."

I called Les, explaining where I was going, and about some breakdown cover for tonight. He had a date, but was still able to cover any calls, then mentioned to him about Kevin and his delight in taking things apart, when there was no need for them to be dismantled.

He said, he would keep an eye on him, also telling him the ladies' car is in one piece, I was getting a drive shaft from the race track tonight or tomorrow.

The three ladies would be coming with me.

Les replied with a disgusting comment, I shrugged it off, "Anyway where is your date for today, they are normally hanging around somewhere"?

"Oh yes, she will be here; she saw what was available last night.'

"Disgusting"

"Oh, I do hope so," Les laughed.

Walking across to the motorhome, the ladies were already carrying their bags from the car to the new location, I hooked up the electric cable and the fresh water connection, then I did a quick check that the systems were working.

I turned on the gas bottle in the van so the water heater would work, and then let the ladies continue to do their thing; it was nearly 10 am in the morning.

I suggested that we leave around three in the afternoon. I said there is a corner shop for anything they may need by the side of the garage.

Digging my hand in my pocket, I pulled out a wad of bank notes, peeling off £20, I passed it to Suzy, you will need this to buy any food and bits required for tonight and tomorrow.

Then I heard a small cough, turned to see, two smiling faces and holding their hands out hoping. The only comment brought was Suzy calling both their full names aloud, they stopped smiling and hurried towards the rear bedroom giggling as they ran.

I estimated her bill for the repair and other charges, and she was with the second-hand parts £25.00 including some staff discount, after all she was cleaning one of the vehicles

Just Three Lads

We had a couple of breakdowns during the day, the final one which started easy then became a nightmare, it involved a fatality, it was a bad crash. With a fatality the Police must get involved, they have set reports to write and sometimes the vehicle is parked out of sight of the public view in a secure storage.
I managed to be all tidied up and finished for just after four.
Les appeared I brought him up to speed what was happening where I would be.

I left him in charge over the weekend, then went to my apartment and changed as I was ordered, I scrubbed up, now I thought should I use lifebuoy soap, or a nice scented French soap I normally use, the French one was always my best choice, then collected my paperwork I required for the trip, popped them into a leather zippy case and picked up my already packed weekend case.

The Motorhome, sparkled in the afternoon sunshine, all the windows were noticeably cleaner, as I climbed in it was clean tidy and smelt lovely, a lady's touch is always best.
Laid on the dashboard was a £50 note, puzzled I asked "Is that your £50,
Suzy replied the girls found it between the cushions and the wall panel.
The girls bright eyed chirped up "Finder's keepers?"
Suzy sharply quelled their enthusiasm that is not ours so just leave the matter alone.
Quickly I replied Ok Ladies are we ready.

A unanimous reply. Yes yes, then a little squeaky voice came out and said be like Elvis and go man go.

I turned to see which little one had come out with that saying, but I only saw two faces the third was hiding behind a cushion.

Adding my reply, Ok Elvis is leaving the building, we go.

Before I made for the main road, I entered the destination into the satellite navigation system in the RV, I drove over to the company diesel pump, then topping up the diesel tank, we headed south.

As we travelled down the A1, I spotted the £50 banknote, reaching over I picked it up, giving it a quick glance, I rubbed it between my fingers, even smelt it. It did have a mildewed whiff.

I looked at Suzy that is Coffin money.

It had been in a damp space or box for a long time.

I folded the note and passed it to Suzy.

Not one of mine, Merry Christmas, share it when you get chance between the girls and yourself.

As Suzy accepted the note, she seemed to jump and immediately cried out, as if she had received an electric shock.

Exclaiming "Oh my!"

What is wrong? I asked,

Replying, I don't know how to say this, when you passed me the note, I had a momentary vision, and heard a voice telling me something.

Wow! What did the voice say?

No, no, it is nothing, let us forget it, and enjoy the weekend.

Suzy had gone white, her smile had gone, she now displayed a worried, confused look. Her children were creating a bit in the back of the RV and she turned and told then firmly to sit and be quiet.

Her reaction startled be somewhat, but also the reaction to the children. Although I had known her only a brief time, with her now widowed and with two children, my memory of her was of a girl, without a care in the world, but she was looking for a life partner.

Sometimes it is best to observe speak when spoken too, I kept my peace this was one of those times.

Peace settled, and the conversation seem to have died, Suzi was deep in thought, the children were a handful but lovely happy little people, I liked them.

Chapter 4

During the drive towards the circuit, the outburst from Suzy was short lived, she went and spoke with the girls in the back of the RV, I watched them in my rear-view mirror, they had a little conference and then Suzy must have told them about my gift of the money and the mood changed again. Taking from what was a small gesture from me had turned another with a problem into the solution.
The girls busied them self selves in the little kitchen, then their activities became reality.
Suzy came forward and standing behind me holding onto the driver's seat, asked did I want to stop for something to eat and drink or continue as we drove along.
I explained I would like to get a little further on before nightfall, but we would be at the race track withing 30 minutes, and threw the decision back for them to decide, I was given a cup of coffee, and a freshly made sandwich again the girls must have been starving, and didn't want to rush me into eating, they were being polite in waiting for me to eat first.

I could get accustomed to this, Suzy told me about herself although now widowed, bringing up two girls was expensive with them wanting to have all the latest gadgets, and designer gear, cash was always tight.

I agreed with her, best to agree than disagree and then the topic of conversation has gone, and the conversation can go on to different things.

The girls had found out how to turn on the TV at the rear of the Motorhome; then sat watching whatever channel they got working.

How old are the Girls?
They are 12 and 13.
Oh dear, the teen years I do not envy you with that task.
Suzy enquired about my status, I confirming my bachelor status, although, girl friends were nice, I liked my space and the freedom.
Freedom, she replied and let out a huge sigh,
Wow, a sigh with regret.
Oops, doom and destruction, wrong word, the flood gates opened and I got the full story.

Luck had it, we were nearly at the race circuit, and I had to cut her short and take note of the directions Doris was telling me, (Doris is what I call my female voice in my Satellite navigation system; she takes me everywhere and does not get me lost).

Pulling into the overnight parking area, I saw a chap waving at me from his campervan, he waved me over,
It was the chap with the driveshaft parking up next to him.

We examined the driveshaft, it was slightly different to the one we had brought, possible it was a modified part, and looked a lot stronger.
but at least Suzy now was back on the road for a

minimum cost, I gave him the fiver he wanted, waved him good bye and we moved onto the paddock.

A bit of fast talking we gained access to the Paddock, I parked slightly back from the rest of the vans,
I started to set up the Motorhome and making it level, it was fun for the girls, they were asking many questions, why do we have to level the Motorhome they asked, so you don't fall out of bed I replied.

The water drains from the sink and shower correctly, when the vehicle is level, impressed or not I got on with the tasks on hand.

Suzy had managed to acquire lots of food to eat, asked was it ok to start cooking the evening meal. I gathered they had not eaten since a hasty snack at breakfast time and the brief snack they had on road as we drove here.

I addressed all the girls, while staying in the RV they are welcome to do and eat what they wish, do not wait to ask me all the time, but if you make a mess clean it up yourself.
I will walk around the Pits see who was here and where they were parked up.

Walking round the pit area, I met up with a few guys, I had not seen for years, invitations to share a few beers, the offer was tempting, I nearly accepted, but I remembered about my guests, declining, I said I would come round later and see them.

Just Three Lads

Returning to a small but excellent basic meal, I asked Suzy if she would like to walk round and see first-hand a group of friends who enjoyed the joys of doing it with one knee on the ground. I got a very puzzled look.

The girls did not want to walk round it was not their scene so they said we could watch TV.

I was unaccustomed to have a female companion with me at a race meeting, we had completed the walk round Suzy not shy of putting the odd drink away, took whatever drinks were offered, she quickly consumed, I kept on coke after the first beer.

The sun had set, the paddock was becoming quiet, racers were also settling into their sleeping bags, as the race is more important with a clear head.

On the way back Suzy stumbled and made a grab for my arm to steady her, she hung on all the way back to the Motorhome.

I think she was a bit tipsy, I made up my bed in the front cabin, she and the girls had taken over the rear bedroom. The girls had found sleeping bags and were tucked in and both fast asleep.

Not wanting to contaminate the interior, with masculine aroma's, I went to the paddock washroom, then returned to the van all was quiet.

I locked the door, and snuggled into my bed, thinking

over the day, and reflecting on the events, I was soon asleep.

I am not sure it seemed liked hours but it probably was minutes, a noise from inside the van woke me, peering outside another camper van had moved alongside, and he was preparing his vehicle for the weekend, most racers do not make too much noise, as they want to be sleeping as well.

Turning round and letting the curtains close behind me, a face in the darkness made me jump. I was face to face with who I thought was Suzy. She held her finger to my lips keeping me from saying anything, and then said very quietly thank you for your kindness, and then kissed me so tenderly her soft lips lingered a little longer than I thought was normal. Yet every kiss is different. I could feel her heart beating, my hands were laid across my chest I could feel her breasts resting on the back of my hands, but there was no warmth in the touch, then as quickly as she appeared she slowing melted into the darkness.

Now you, might as well smack me round the ear with a wet fish after a meeting like that, and in the darkness too. I was wide-awake, the idea of sleep was the last thing on my mind. Sitting up in bed, my ears listening intensely for any sound, after a while, nothing unusual, the gentle breathing from the children and Suzy were the only noises.
Not sure the meaning, I gave the thank you kiss, some thought, I would quiz Suzy in the morning then I drifted

off into a deep sleep.

A rider taking his race bike to the scrutinising tent, woke me, some noises are not common in daily life, one such noise is the noise from race brake discs, they click or rattle as they are slowly rolled along. Initially until you know what this noise is your ears become attuned to it, that bike passed followed by more bike's each rattling a story as they rolled by.

One chap started his race bike, the deep grunting boom of the single cylinder resounded around the pits. These racers never really grew up and they love the noise their bikes make and are extremely willing to share, with everyone.
Once one engine starts, it becomes the invitation for all the engines to start up and make their claim on a bit of the morning silence.
Mechanics and riders, were starting their engines, revving them to warm them as quickly as they can, the paddock starts to have a distinct aroma of burning engine oil gives the paddock area a smell, that only flourishes at the race circuits of the world.
Then the public address system booms a message. First race practice, competitors to the paddock holding area.

Race day had started.

Screams of 'What the hell is that bloody noise,' emitted from the bedroom at the rear of the cabin.
My guests are awake,

Just Three Lads

Good morning, ladies, I replied to their question.

I was dressing when the dividing curtain was urgently opened, a scantily clad female made a beeline for the loo, No number twos in the loo.
Please use the loo in the Pit area.
'Oh shit' came back the reply a tea shirt was thrown into the half open door then a nearly fully clad female, hurried towards the paddock washroom and loo.

I am glad I said that, thinking it isn't nice cleaning up after somebody, but rules are rules, then another body heading in the same direction took off across the grass, a friendly voice from outside said anymore doing this run it is entertaining?

I managed to get out van between the run of female bodies back and forth, judging by the cloudless blue sky today was going to be a scorcher. as my guests dashed back, the cold was telling on their sticky out parts.

As I was up, I rechecked the electric cable connecting suppling the van with electricity we had enough water to ensure the guests had enough to have a light shower, and prepare for the day ahead.

Opening the side door to the RV I requested permission for a lonely male to enter his domain? A reply from deep withing the van suggested, safer in ten minutes make it fifteen and you should be perfectly safe.

Geordie an old friend had parked up next to my van,

waved a cup indicating there was coffee on offer.

An invitation not to be wasted, I sauntered over towards his site, his lovely wife Kate was already preparing me a cup.

Kate enquired,
"Not race goers then?"
"I don't know, I only met them yesterday"
Her mouth opened spluttering,
"Yesterday, really yesterday, hey guy, now I am impressed."

Chapter 5

Thanks for the coffee, I ambled back to my van.

As I opened the door, the aroma of cooked bacon and toast wafted past my nose, something very tasty was being prepared on the grill,

I called out, good mornings, and permission to come on board?

A multi voiced good morning greeted me as I entered the van,

Suzy asked "Is this normal, all this noise at a race meeting noise; noise and more noise?"

"Yes, I am afraid so, unfortunately where we parked, we are in the thick of it."

"Oh dear, we thought it all started at 1 o clock like the TV," Suzy replied, then enquired,

"Did I like bacon egg, sausage, with beans on toast?"

"Oh Yes, I will survive all day with that meal," and that is exactly what was placed in front of me.

More toast to follow if required.

The girls sat down at the table, the younger one sidled up to me, then demolished their breakfast, the little one asked what happens here? As she slurped on her glass of milk.

I went on to explain about the bikes, the riders, and the racers that participate, together with other stuff that happens, it can be a family type of atmosphere but there are nasties.

A chorus repeated the word, Nasty.

Just Three Lads

I explained within the paddock is everything your little hearts will desire, look round take it all in, do not get involved or accept anything from some riders, they may appear to be friendly. Just be careful where you are walking, remember race bikes do not move for you, you give way to them and other vehicles.
If in doubt, stay out, then come find your mum or me quickly.
I gave each of them one of my business cards keep that in your pocket, if anyone asks, you are with me.
You know where the Motorhome is, the door will not be locked.
Ok. Was the reply, whether they heeded the warnings, I will never know, they departed from the van and went forth looking for things that may be of interest to them.

A fresh brew of coffee, was placed in front of me, Suzy then sat down across the table.
Then taking chance impulsively, quizzed me about my history, why I had not been married, who was the female in my life?
Doris is the only female in my life.
Reacting, where was Doris now?
She is sat on the dashboard I replied,
The puzzled look was brilliant, I noticed her eyes move quickly as she glanced at the dashboard.
She is not! Then she stared at me again, this time, with a cheeky grin.
I think she realised I was pulling her leg, (I wish; it was a nice leg, in fact they were both nice) Replying she is the female voice in the Satellite Navigation system, she is the only lady, I have been serious friends with for over

ten years, Doris always, gets me to the correct place on time and safely, she has saved me from Police radar traps, and speed camera's.

She is a dear.

Suzy continuing the third degree, asked How long have you had this Motorhome?

I have owned for a few years but only finished the repair two weeks ago so this is the first trip I have made in it.

'What repair? She looked confused, as she could see no damage; I explained where the accident happened pointing to certain parts and the area around where the driver sat. there was slight accident damage to the offside corner but a projectile entered the cabin through the windscreen.

Les did the repair in our workshop. We never knew exactly who it belonged to just a company name on the documents, I believe a member of the family came and removed some of the personal items, a lot of lady's stuff was removed. little bits turned up here and there, I think they are in a draw somewhere.

The little draw in the corner, I found them when cleaning, the girls found them first, I told them to leave them as we were not sure who they belonged to, and we were guests and should not touch anything or say anything about things found however strange or perverted.

Perverted stuff? Oh dear, best not tell Kevin, about them or he will be confused.

I started to laugh, and sneezed, I requiring a tissue, I made a move for the toilet to get some toilet roll.

Just Three Lads

Coming back, I asked "Why did you come and kiss me last night and say thank you?"
Suzy replied "Pardon! I did no such thing,"
I am sure I did not imagine it, but it was dark, I was tired, "I could have been dreaming."
Thinking No, I am sure, when I felt lips on mine and breasts pressing on to my hands, I am not dreaming.

Suzy was fascinated now enquired, what did this female do?
Well let me see, I had got into my bed, and had closed my eyes, then hearing a noise from outside of the van, I moved a curtain, to see what it was.
Just another camper, I then settling into my bed, then I felt this van creak, as if somebody, was moving around.
looking for anyone moving, I saw this face coming towards me, it came close enough to put a finger on my mouth, as if to stop me from saying anything.
Then the vision came closer and gave me a passionate kiss.
My hands were on my chest, then I felt the softness of her breasts as they laid on the back of my hands.
I may add, I had no feeling of warmth.
Suzy replied "Oh my God".
The vision seemed to disappear into the darkness.
Then I was wide awake for at least an hour, in case she came back.
Well, I can assure you, that I did not do anything like that last night, neither would the girls.
All I can say, you asked, I told it like it happened.

Just Three Lads

If I did do such a thing, I would most certainly have some clothes on; I do not know you well enough to do such an act naked.
Please don't mention this to the Girls.
I would not even consider it; the girls have their own thoughts and ideas.
Suzy smiled as she thanks me,

It was a different voice I replied,
What do you mean?
You said thank you and it was not the same voice.

It was a.., sorry I cannot describe the voice, but it was not the same.
Suzy, intrigued by these revelations, bombarded me with more questions; show me where you were.
I reset the table area, into the bed layout and took my position as I was laid.
I heard the voice from that direction, my hand indicating the spot, Suzy went and stood in the same place,
What happened next?
The image moved towards me, Suzy reacting as I spoke, yes, that is about correct, then a finger or was it two, I wasn't sure on that point was placed across my lips.
A voice said Thank you!
Suzy placed one finger than added another finger on my lips, then said Thank you.
No, the finger was vertical, as if saying shush to a child.
She repeated the finger gesture then said thank you,
That was very close. Suzy leant forward and put her lips on mine; as she pulled away, a door of the overhead

locker dropped down hitting Suzy on the back of her head.

Oh dear, she cried jumping back a pace, how did that happen?

She quickly moved her hand over her face, hair, and head where the locker door had hit her. She looked at her hand there was no blood, but did feel a little bump on the back of her head.

Looking at the door, it was held closed by a magnetic catch, making the door was either open or closed.

It could not be in such a position to fall open.

Maybe I had missed some damage when the repair was done. I went round, opened, and closed all the cupboard and locker doors, even tested the sliding doors.

I made sure this was not likely to happen again.

The outside door burst open, in flew two very excited girls, both in full flow of what they had seen, and people they had talked too, they had seen racers going so fast, they had to put their knee on the ground to stop them falling off.

I explained it wasn't to stop falling off it was a style of riding that was popular today when going very fast round corners.

Suzy holding her chin in her hand, replied, Men doing it with one knee on the floor. now I understand what you meant.

I bet you were thinking something else.

You mentioned, I would not kiss you naked, when we were discussing the phantom, because you did not know me that well.

Just Three Lads

Does that mean if you get to know me better, that you would?
I got that staring look, plus the reply, "Might do".
Then she replied, and you stayed awake waiting for her to come back, before falling asleep.

Chapter 6

I have had enough inquisition, with the start of race practice, the excitement I clamoured was happening outside, playing around with a ghost, vision, or apparition, can be investigated, later, the mysterious woman present or deceased wasn't my idea of fun.

Looking out of the window, I spoke, I am off to have a walk around, watch the race bikes; if anyone wanting to join me better get their backsides together and move.

Three followed me from the van, walking towards the old hairpin I saw a program on the ground, picking it up it was for this meeting, sitting on the grass embankment, I browsed through the program making note of which rider displayed what number.

It was a good day sunny no wind at all. The peace was shattered with the distance rumble from the bike's exhaust as they sped away from the holding bay, a mixed bunch of bikes taking it easy on the initial lap, each rider checking his bike also the switched-on riders checking the track surface, for any obstacle to evade when they were in race mode.

Watching the group proceed down the hill virtually in silence, until they were nearby, as they passed, the exhaust screams and roars produced by various engines used in race bikes, it was in a way, music to my ears. Not so much music but a huge din as they passed the Suzy and the girls were, holding their ears trying to cut down the excruciating noise.

Hold on I said, then searching in my jacket finding a few

packets of earplugs. Passing them out then I showed them how to inset them.

The next lap, the exhaust noise subdued was easier to enjoy. Suzy asks why different noises came from virtually the same looking bike.

I tried to explain the different engines to her but distractions from the two girls made the explanations hard to understand. It was easier to let them watch and answered only questions, I was asked, and then in the simplest of terms.

After an hour, the Tannoy announced the lunch break, I started back towards our camp; walking past the burger van, I mentioned, who would like a burger, or hot dog with chips?

A unanimous Yes, it was quick and easy way of feeding walking dustbins.

Meandering around the paddock, a friendly face ambled towards me and started chatting about the races and who did I think would be the winner.

He had walked in between myself and Suzy, she was not pleased, passing a few names to the friend, we agreed that at this meeting it was a one or two horse race.

Suzy asking how could that be? My friend realised that I had a companion with me, and he apologised profusely for butting in, I dispelled his apology and introduced him to Suzy turning around to include the children but they were not to be seen.

Going back to Suzie's question, local knowledge, and a fast bike, would be the contributory factor.

But lookout for the dark horse, there is always one, he would follow the main group, plan his moves from the back and take advantage of any mistakes made by the super heroes. Many a race has been lost by the winner celebrating before the flag drops.

A few other faces appeared, some guys asking if I have a part for this and a bit for that;

they would bell me next week to find out. Suzy came and stood close and held onto my upper arm, I felt her jump as the Tannoy announced the start of the races, and calling all competitors to the assemble area.

Then the Tannoy thundered again the final call for Race one.

It was time to go to our favourite part of the circuit to watch the first race we stood on the first corner always a site of excitement or carnage.

The lights changed and the race was off, again the silence as the bikes approached the corner a full grid all arriving at a righthand corner is an impressive picture, as not everyone gets the correct line, then they must prepare for the downhill section and a hairpin corner, where we standing before lunch, where are your children I asked Suzy. They went back to the camper, to watch TV.

My attention was redirected to leading group, the Tannoy giving some information of a bike off the track, the leaders name eluded me, with another unknown name very close behind, we watched them as they weaved and tried all tactics to gain a better position, to be first across the finish line.

They passed us again, good grouping for the second lap, and the third by the fourth the field starting to string-out,

Just Three Lads

Reminding Suzy that it was a two-horse race, I pointed out the two riders involved, and the dark horse now in third position and gaining on the second man

That rider is shadowing but keeping up easily with the leaders, it's easier to follow the leaders, then analyse the leaders' tactics, than make dive for the front and keep there for the full race unless you have a quick machine.

The race was down, to the last lap the front two had changed places many times, the third man creeping closer, as the group rounded the last corner, the third man made his move, he tried a late braking manoeuvre, which brought him and bike into a tight group and contention, this caught the second man out, our black horse gained second place, the leader expecting a challenge, pointed for the finish line and kept accelerating hard, managed to keep him behind to the chequered flag.

Suzy was furious, he can't do that can he?

First under the linen is the winner providing you are not riding in a reckless manner and he was leading when the third man made his move. Immediately the race control over the speaker system called for competitors for race two.
Not a race I wished to watch but if Suzy and the girls wished to, I did not mind. The girls were nowhere to be seen, then I remembered Suzy said they had gone back to the motorhome to watch TV.

Just Three Lads

The lost lonely cloud in all but perfect sky managed to shield the warmth of sun's rays from us, I was feeling a chill, Suzy she required a call of nature, suggesting a return to the paddock.

Making our way back Suzy linked arms with me, probably a rider would not make me move but a female was fair game, something I never thought anything of at the time yet, a couple of riders wives I was on speaking terms with; had observed the linked arms move, waved tea cups a standard procedure in a noisy paddock to invite you to join them for a cup of tea or coffee.

Thinking about it now the sudden burst of invites, was them being nosey so they could find out any gossip, who was this lady with me. I think I even referred to Suzy at the time, they are being nosy and will ask many questions. I think I can take care of myself she replied I have had good training. but did not elaborate on her reply.

Approaching the ice cream van, I remarked, "Do you fancy one?"

'Oh yes please,' she replied,

"What about an ice cream?" that would be nice too, Suzy replied.

'Lovely' I replied I had used that joke for years; I see that you have a sharpness like me.

Suzy replied, I am a quick learner, pausing as she licked her ice cream.

This vision you saw last night, can you tell me more?

Not really, I thought it was you, but as you said it wasn't I believe you and it wasn't one of the girls their face was too young. but I am confident it happened, after she (the vision) had gone, I was wide awake and savoured the few seconds over again, I even found it stimulating in a strange way.

Strange? Suzy asked.

Stimulating if you really want to know, I do not generally talk as open as this, especially with people I have just met. This for me is slightly uncomfortable.

Suzy looked at me and suggested sitting down a small table close to the ice cream van. We can watch the racing and chat as well, she went on to say that, she understands that I am uncomfortable with the developing situation, but she is really interested in the phenomenon that I am experiencing.

Her mother had claimed, she had this gift of being able to see and talk with spirits; but I never understood what she told me, she always saw another side to the story.

Suzy moved her head towards me beckoning me to do the same, kissing me on my lips. She then pulled back, and looked around, as if waiting for something to happen.

Interesting, the last time I kissed you, I was attacked by a locker door, now nothing has happened how strange.

Something had happened but I wasn't telling her, I had experienced an erection, I was glad I was sitting down I managed to hide my problem by leaning forward.

The Tannoy thundered out that the big race of the day was being called.

This is what I came to see, I stood up looking for a good place to go and watch, Suzy also noticed what I was hiding, rearranged the race program to distract any other observation.

Just Three Lads

We walked over to the fence to get an uninterrupted view, Suzy slipped her short jacket off and asked me to hold it, an unusual request but I was glad of the extra article to hold in front of me.

The race gantry strip of red start lights were all brightly lit, the bike engines revving to maximum, the lights extinguished, and twenty racing bikers, all heading for the same spot on the first corner, the bikes all being of similar power the group will tend to arrive together, the faster men will be first in and first out, the not so brave will ease the throttle back and relegate themselves to the following pack, the roar of exhausts from the pack as they now accelerates away to wards the next corner; with us standing behind them, we received the full noise blast until the throttle closes for the next corner and the bikes take another direction following the circuit, we were still able to watch the leaders from our position as they challenged each other for the lead, trying every trick in the book to gain an advantage.

As the laps counted down, the three riders from the previous race, took the lead, the third rider Suzy's favourite dark horse rider shadowing the front two much closer, as they passed, I listened to his engine revs although trying he was matching the leaders speed and track position while he worked his final plan of attack.
How, when and where he would try to make this his race. On the last lap and the trio of riders virtually inside each other's fairings you would need a set of feeler gauges to measure the gap between them.

Just Three Lads

The second to the final corner was when the second man made a move and collided with the leader's rear wheel, causing them both to run wide as they tried to recover from the collision, third man also forced into the run off area, his bike went down on gravel and he was thrown off his bike.

The fourth fifth and sixth man took over the lead and the podium positions.

Wow now that's was a turn up for the books I said. I bet they are surprised, and with the prize money on offer a welcome bonus for their expenses.

Suzy ecstatic was jumping up and down and shouting for the winners.

"Do you always get this excited at race meetings"?

That was the most exciting thing I have ever watched I did not realise that motorcycle racing was as exciting as that."

It can get better and it can get worse when all riders get up and walk away unhurt that is the good time, pointing towards the ambulance at the start finish line tending to the fallen riders, when they announce that they are ok then it is good and the crowd is happy.

Let's go and see what happened only to be found first hand from the other riders.

Walking towards the pits Suzy was hanging on my arm happy with her day so far, she gave my arm a hug and stretched up and kissed me on the cheek.

What was that for? Just, a little thank you for helping us. She replied and taking and putting her jacket on.

Searching for the expert that knows of all devious mischief in the paddock, I found Geordie with cup in hand Kate was already pouring another cup, she just poured another cup and passed it to Suzy, Geordie was in good spirits, he said that his bike had got a second place and the prize is very welcome.

Suzy asked to be excused disappearing towards the washroom.

Kate immediately started to give me the third degree, who were the female with luggage in tow?

Explaining I was helping them get somewhere; she should not read too much into the situation.

Geordie and I became involved in a deep discussion re the motorhome.

I had told him before; I had an accident damaged one in for repair; gesturing towards the RV next to his. is the final article.

It is ok, apart for a couple of teething problems. Then I noticed Kate doing something in the back of their race van, she kept looking out making sure nobody could see, then she removed her blouse, then her bra, she turned to get a new top, giving me an outstanding view, then slowly swung her tits at me, with a laugh, she slipped on her new top.

I reckoned that performance was for my benefit as Suzy returned, she surveyed the scene, asking what happens next. I jokingly replied, if I was in Geordies position humping.

Suzy gave me a quizzical look.

Kate's pale skin started to tinge with a bit of colour, as we returned to our camp, I mentioned Kate must be a village girl her nipples were standing out like chapel hat pegs.

Just Three Lads

A memorable image for me, her embarrassment as soon as she realised, picked up a kettle and held it close to cover her excitement.

Chapter 7

I turned to Suzy and asked what would you like for tea?
Quickly replying is this a trick question like the ice
cream one?
Giving me a wide eyed but with a mischievous look.

Suppose that's me told I replied.
Let's as what the girls would like I am quite happy with
something from the burger van or the fish and chip shop.

A blast of hot air flew passed me, as I entered the
motorhome, oh my word, it was like a sauna, both girls
were flat out on sofa beds, the TV switched on and the
volume was loud.

I found it was stuffy reacting I open the roof hatch,
which opened easily.
The heating was on full, a warning bell ringing in my
head was to, get those children out of here, now, Suzy
grabbed the little one, I took hold of the elder one and
carried her outside and sat them on the grass, I think
there has been an excess of carbon monoxide inside the
home.

Opening all the windows wide and I shut off the heating
although it set under midway, maybe it the heating was
never checked as the repair was done during the early
part of the year it may have been never checked.

Just Three Lads

Geordie's daughter saw the two girls sitting on the grass
and came over to chat to them.
She looked at me and said are they ok?
Yes, I think so, why?
One has been sick on the grass,
Suzy hearing this looked at her, her eyes looked strange
as she looked back at me,
Geordie's daughter ran and told Geordie, he immediately
ran into his caravan, grabbed a few items ran he had with
him a carbon monoxide tester in his hand.
He placed it in the motorhome, he left it in there to get a
reading, he quickly came out outside.
Looking at one, he said bring the other one quickly and
picked up one girl, I picked up the other, and we headed
for the paddock medical tent.
Geordie not waiting on ceremony strode straight into the
tent, the doctors seeing us carrying two little ones,
Geordie remarked, "Possible Carbon monoxide
poisoning" and laid one of the girls on the bed. I
followed and laid the other girl beside her;
Suzy followed us into the tent, hand to mouth looking
deathly white.
Both the Doctor and nurse both sprang into action,
checking vital signs,
the nurse asked us to leave then allowed mum to stay.

Geordie said let's have a look at that motorhome of
yours, as we walked back, we chatted, he had found in
one caravan he had purchased, blocked air vents, a
leaking fridge joint and what was the most dangerous a
hole in the gas exhaust from the cooker, and that blasted

thing was able to leak into the cabin, there are so many amateurs bodge this equipment it is untrue.

The carbon monoxide tester was reading dangerous levels, that was after I had opened the roof vent and left the front door open, Geordie pointing at the roof vent are you sure, it was closed, and the lock down catches were in place.
He looked round and found a tea towel had slipped down over the cooker air vent, then a sleeping bag was stuffed into the back of the seat, closing off the rear vent.
The only one left to check, was the front facing vent this is was near the driver's seat, placing my hand down near the grill, I could not feel a draught.
Geordie was already outside looking into the vent, and he found another problem, this vent was taped over, Geordie swung under the front bumper and stretched his hand and arm up the back of the front radiator grill, it was covered in masking tape, put there by the painter to stop any over spray going into the cabin area.
I was sure that we would have removed the tape before fitting radiator grill.
Saying to Geordie, as I was driving up, I remember a draught from that vent was nice.
Geordie went back inside and removed the vent inner panel, shining a light into the hole, there should have been a bridging tube that would connect the two vents, but that is the original vent hole that panel wasn't changed.
We kept digging then we found the problem,
We worked out the inside vent panel, could be fitted two ways, simply removing the plate, and turning it over, the

plate aligned, refitting the screws in their holes vent was now fixed.

Geordie remarked, I think you have been lucky.

We intend sleeping in here again tonight, but I think it would be safer if all the gas and any causes of danger be removed or disconnected.

He helped me disconnect the gas pressure regulator to the gas tank, we left the electric hook-up be the only form of power going into the motorhome.

Geordie left the monoxide tester to keep a check overnight, saying that it has a high-pitched buzzer that will let you know if the Co, fume levels go high again, I have two Co, meters in my van so keep that one in here on loan mind.

We checked more things on the motorhome, all seem to be in order, I talked about the repair I did and the damage was minimal this could be down to the manufacture he remarked, it will be worth a call and have them check it later in the week.

Agreed we walked over to the medical tent two little girls one woman were the same shade of, off white, the Doc saying we have given them oxygen and they have perked up a lot, did you find the problem with the van?

We think we have two vents were covered and one had self-closed but we have removed the gas bottle so no gas is in the van.

Suzy starting to pick up a bit and Geordie saying c'mon and have some tea with us and some fresh air too much sitting around in places watching TV is bad for you.

Geordie's daughter was waiting for the girls to come back and started chatting as girls do, all seemed to be forgotten as they ran off to do something.

Just Three Lads

Suzy still shocked talked with Geordie's wife sipping on a cup of tea.
How badly damaged was the van? Geordie enquired,
I lowered my voice to a whisper, to make sure Suzy didn't hear, it had a slight front end, the main damage was on the driver's side, evidently the vehicle when parking up, ran into the back of an already parked wagon, and that was loaded with an overhanging girder, the girder entered the van through the screen and pinned the driver in his seat.

We never found out if there was anyone else in the van.

Someone came the next day, and removed all items of value. They left the general silly bits of junk, we found over the time, as we were repairing it.
But it was an easy repair, it is a pleasure to drive, so I thought I might hang on to it.

Chapter 8

Geordie invited us to join them for a barbecue.

"Yes" was a spontaneous reply. Came from the female side of the team.

Suzy suggested that she could bring the food we were going to prepare for our evening meal.

We collected what was needed and went and joined the party outside in the dusk.

Geordie already had the brazier glowing with lots of meat cooking, Sausages and other tasty morsels were waiting to be cooked.

The girls were chatting, getting to know each other were having a great time.

Geordie's wife in deep discussion with Suzy, was telling her more about motorcycle racing and what goes on, probably a few other secrets that ladies talk about.

Those times when the guys are deep in discussion and removing the ring pulls from the cans of drink. The girls seem to be happy with a bottle of wine, that Kate had hidden.

Fresh paddock gossip around the campfires, was brisk and can get very detailed amongst riders and mechanics sometimes leaving the ladies cold. Reflecting on their choice of men in the early days would it have been different if they had not followed motorsport.

The food was delicious and as it was getting to pudding time, Geordie appeared from the caravan with a bunch of Banana's anyone fancy a barbecued Banana?

Silence no acceptance, nobody has tried one, placing two on the grill he cooked them in their skins until one side went black, then flipping it over cooked the other side, placing them on plates he cut open from one end to another, put a spoon on a plate and said taster's.

Be careful they are very hot inside, wow I tasted a spoon full and instantly said I will have a full one.

Possibly with another bottle of beer.

The entire hand of Bananas was quickly cooked and consumed.

Leaving all who indulged a feeling of contentment.

More people joined the party and discussions became varied and fragmented, the evening air was becoming cold,

Suzy chased the girls of to bed, she sat close to me enjoying the warmth from the fire, Geordie put on a couple more logs and the flames grew and sparks started to rise in the air.

"Not a good idea that with all the bikes and high-octane fuel around" I whispered.

No problem, he replied, sliding a fine metal mesh across the top of the brazier the heat still penetrating, the sparks ceased rising.

Discussions starting to wane,

Suzy whispered "I am off to my bed, see you in the morning," kissed my ear she walked briskly of to the motorhome.

Geordie quizzed me about the female and instant family?

I explained the problem with her car and her need to get to a meeting in the big city.

Deciding I was feeling the cold I said "I am off to my bed as well,"

"Your bed, Geordie remarked

"Yes! My bed, I replied. "See you in the morning,"

"I don't think so, we will be up, and gone very early, long way to go, jobs to do on the way."

"Ok" I replied "see you whenever."

Kate gave me a big hug spreading her chest into mine, she whispered "You can see more if you like."

I thanked her for sharing their food and company tonight after such a dramatic day, I didn't wish to add more conflict to an already complicated day, leaving it at that I sauntered towards my Motorhome.

Spending another night in the RV would be interesting, the interior smelt fresher and looking at the Co meter it displayed all levels were safe within the cabin, I started to get undressed, and just as I managed to get my PJs on Suzy knocked on the wall and asked could she come and see me.

Yes, I would like that, and invited her into my space,

She came and sat beside me on my bed, and whispered, I am concerned and worried.

Tell me your problem and if I can help I will. She said did I fancy a drink? Oh, I replied that would be nice, she brought two glasses and a small bottle of a Scottish whiskey I had never heard of, and emptied the bottle into two glasses.

We have no ice as I forgot to make any, that's ok I replied.

Suzy had the floor, and she told me about this weekend how it was frightening and fantastic, and her worry was her children, she said the little one has been taken by you, as she has not had male figure to be with for such a long time.

I like the little one also in fact I quite like the entire family, without any favourites. I too was horrified how easy it could have been to have had a serious accident today, but also, we had left them unattended in a strange vehicle, had either one of us been with them it might have been another story, and we would not be here having a board of enquiry.

Suzy took a sip from her glass and leant forward kissing me on my lips, I did notice that she has very soft lips, she then laid her head on my shoulder and snuggled into me.

My thoughts were how lovely what a nice way to end what could be a perfect weekend, alas it was not to be. I simply fell asleep.

I woke in the morning Suzy was cooking breakfast, and the children were in the back reading books.

The whisky glasses had been washed and put away, during breakfast, I was annoyed with myself for falling asleep, Suzy did not refer to the evening discussion so I left it there. Knowing that if we wanted to talk again there hopefully was no problem, to interfere.

Chapter 9

Before we started, Suzy gave me the address we would be driving to in the city; I entered these details, into Doris's database. it is comforting when driving on crowded roads and streets, one little service like this in a car can save the day, also I would receive warning of any speed or a redlight cameras. the persistence of sneaky county councils makes to extort money from the already over taxed motorists, there is an industry out there working exclusively for the benefit of the driver.

Suzy and the girls had to be there for a certain time, parking for a motorhome was virtually impossible, so I intended to drop them off, find a parking space, walk to, and meet up with them at that office.

Or I could hang around in the street, watching the people and the secretary's flitting back and forth, or if available sit in a small café and wait for them there.

Suzy pointed out the office building as it came into view, she had never mentioned the purpose of her meeting, and I was not of an inquisitive nature. The three hurried off, I continued to find a parking place, I remembered a few blocks away, a. old mate that had a garage in the town, parking might be easier there.

I was just about to drive on the garage forecourt, when the stupid van conked out.

C'mon old girl, don't do this to me. I will give you an oil change when we get back. That temptation didn't help neither, she sat and laughed at me, and she still would not respond, I always talked to my vehicles and gave them ladies names, then if they do have a spirit then they may like the offhand chat. Nope. she had stopped, she would not go, the engine cranked over ok, so I put the transmission into 1st gear and pulled the van onto the forecourt using the power of the starter motor; it was slow going but, inch by inch she advanced onto the forecourt, that trick I would only perform in a dire emergency, it helps when you are on your own but there is a down side, you could burnout the starter, then as if by magic she started. I was back in control and drove the van sedately onto the forecourt, I manoeuvred the RV around the back of the garage, parked her up, and went to see my old friend.

John Wade, motor dealer extraordinaire and the kind of guy you count your fingers after shaking hands with.

'Good morning what brings you to my door so early on this fine morning, and good to see you again." he held out his hand.

Just a social call, I replied, and a favour to park the motorhome, I must pick somebody up in an hour.

Was that you cranking that beast onto the forecourt one of the mechanic guys spotted you,

Unfortunately, yes it was, that van has been a problem this weekend, I gave him a brief explanation of the events. He thought and replied 'Christine' the van is a Christine.

What the fuck, is a Christine?

He went on to say, there was film where an old car fell in love with that geek of a kid, then the kid got a girlfriend, Christine, the car, tried to kill her, then when the kid tried to protect the girl from the car, it tried to kill him.

I was stunned with his reply, I had heard of this film but I had not had chance to watch it.

I replied, whatever you are you smoking I suggest replacing it with a new weed.

John offered as his lads were available, they can put Christine over the pit, and see it we can see anything for you. Then suggested go get yourself over to that meeting and will see you when you get back.

Ok throwing the keys towards him be careful with Doris, Aha We got a Doris.

Where is the meeting, John enquired "At company called Hardy Able & Sangster they are based in Champion Street?

Now I didn't notice but johns face changed and he paused for breath a little bit longer than normal, then replied with a warning. Watch out for that bunch of crooks, John ferociously replied, those bastards, did me on a few services, they always try to find a rattle or problem and refuse to pay the bill.

and rattled off a couple of tricks they pull, they are past experts in the charge, and invoice padding, if they got you £10,000, they would incur a charge odd or even, depending on the day or time.

That was an old mid-century rip off; thought it died out...

People and newspaper forget John replied.

Ok will catch up when I get back.

Heading in the direction of Champion Street I walked through the back streets although a short cut, one can also observe what cars are parked up in private car parks. I saw a large bold sign for Hardy Abel and Sangster Private Parking offenders <u>will be towed</u> away. I noticed the line under the Will be Towed, was hand painted and a shaky hand as well. The sign did make a statement.

I turned the corner, and had to flatten myself against the back wall, a large black German car swept into the alleyway, didn't even slow, the car turned into the H.A.& S car park. one of the directors I thought.

Walking towards the front entrance I strolled down the street until I had reached their office.

An impressive front on an old building, it screamed expense, how do they manage to make money, I surmised they could not stand an in-depth investigation.

Entering reception, I was greeted by a young girl, dressed to the nines, she obviously oversaw the reception desk.

How may I help you she enquired, I have come to pick up Mrs Suzy, I am sorry I do not know here last name, also her children, when they are ready.

Oh yes, please take a seat, they shouldn't be very long.

Taking a seat, I sat looking towards a closed door with sign on the front saying Accounts.

Asking the receptionist if I could use the facilities, she pointed in the direction of the location.

Suddenly my telephone rang, wishing to keep it quiet I switched it off; not realising I had pressed the record button for the built-in camera. I slid the phone into my top pocket of my jacket on the chair I was sitting on, another door it opened, and another chap dressed in a well-tailored blueish black suit, came out then spoke swiftly with the receptionist, I heard her reply he is the taxi driver for Mrs Suzy. he entered the accounts office in front of my seat, I had an unprecedented view of what was going on.

Not wishing to be nosey I left my coat on the chair and went to the toilet.

When I came back the receptionist said that Mrs Suzy will be with you in a minute.

Thank you I replied, recovering my jacket I noticed the red light indicating the camera was recording, I pressed the button and stopped the camera recording then slid the phone back into my shirt pocket.

Suzy and the girls came out Suzy looking a bit down the children spotted me and ran over to me, the little one taking hold of my hand. I looked at her and whispered "Den" she replied Den and she nodded her head.

Was everything ok?

Suzy was looking a bit Shakey, Yes and No, but I must accept the outcome, the lady from the office came out with a cheque in hand and asking Suzy could she sign her receipt book.

Just then a large chap with very red-faced burst in through the front door, his entrance certainly impressive, he looked around and demanded to see Sangster! This new man's arrogance cleared a path in front of him, he was full of Woe, and in loud voice claiming blue murder and then, what he wasn't going to do to these crooks had not been written yet.

Suzy grabbed the eldest girl close to her, keeping out of this new man mountains way. The little one saw her mum grip intensify on her sister, she also reacted holding my hand tighter and moved by the side of the chair placing me in between her and this new blustering giant.

As Suzy was preparing to signed her receipt book, Man Mountain excused himself towards Suzy, saying in a quiet but pleasant voice, "Oh please excuse me I am disturbing your business with these charlatan's, he observed the cheque going into the envelope, then replied I would check the details these bastards have been known to write dud cheques." the lady placed a cheque in a new envelope and passed it to Suzy.

Suzy immediately extracted the cheque from the envelope and scanned the details written upon, then passed it back to the office lady she declared, "The date is incorrect. could I have a new cheque and one without mistakes."

The office lady now had been caught out immediately did her bidding and returned with a corrected cheque, this was inspected to Suzy's satisfaction only then we left the office. Both children now were holding onto me, the giant now simmering nicely was waiting for his meeting, then Suzy did an unpredictable action she walked up to this man thanked him for his advice and stood and placed a kiss on his cheek.

A door in the end of the corridor opened and two burly men appeared, took one look at our gentle giant, and retreated.

Our gigantic hero, boomed out again it is Sangster, I want to see, I know he is here, so keep your steroid twin's well away from me.

By this time the little one was so wide eyed to her it was important to keep me between herself and the disturbance.

Whether he achieved his demands or not is unknown to me as Suzy wished to get out of there as fast as she could.

Walking briskly away I remarked, good lord, never had I ever been in such a heated meeting as that, even some of the stand off's I have experienced with the label of fault being decided by the roadside at the accident sites are never as heated as that.

I was curious now I wanted to know the outcome of the meeting between those two, and I chuckled to myself at the term "the steroid twins" and I imagined the state of confusion that office would be in now.

Suzy replied. The way I feel, I would have done the same.

Now you tell me if you wish but I won't enquire, your business is your business.

We walked along the road talking about anything but what she had just experienced.

As we approached the Wades garage, Suzy said I know this garage, Jim her deceased husband had something to do with it.

The next hour would prove to be very interesting, or so I thought.

Well do you want to come in or not,

No, she replied We will wait over there in that Happy burger bar and will come and meet you when you drive out of the garage.

I slipped Suzy £10 to get something for your lunches and gave her a kiss on the cheek, then I started walking towards, Wades workshop, the motorhome was over the main pit, Wade underneath and looking and prodding for something.

What's up I called and let myself down into the pits.

Oh, err nothing, I wish you had gone into reception, and not walked into the garage, you're not insured in here.

My immediate response to that statement was you cheeky bugger, we have virtually the same sized garage and conduct a lot more dangerous work than you do.

He mumbled on; we were just checking your van for problems.

I asked what have you found?

To be honest nothing but these, and held up a pair of diesel sodden ladies' knickers, one of the lads pulled these out of the diesel tank, and some clear plastic strips, and a plastic carrier bag, also there was water in the diesel.

We drained the tank and all this crap floated out, the plastic bag probably blocked the fuel pickup pipe and stopped the engine.

I agreed with him that was the probable cause of the breakdown. John then seemed to switch from a hostile to a friendly mode, enquired further So you never touched the bottom of the van?

Nope, just repaired the front corner where the Girder came through the screen.

Cool as, murmured John, now in deep thoughts, may I ask is this vehicle up for sale?

"It might be later as this is the first trip out. I hadn't decided.

I wasn't even coming this way, to day I offered to drop a colleague off for a meeting."

Just Three Lads

John blurted out; Yes, yes, so you said but, Can I have first refusal when you do?

I will remember and call you when I decide.
Fair doo's Wade replied.
I remarked what do I owe you?
You need diesel, what was in the tank was a suspect diesel, there was some contamination mixed in, so just fill it up at my pump and we will call it even.
Ok sounds a good deal to me. I wish I had checked his price first, but it was a deal I may have spent an hour looking for that problem on the side of the road, the fuel tanks topped up fired "Christine" up and headed out of there. I approached the happy burger bar three happy smiling figures ran to the side of the road, they boarded quickly we were on our way again.
Little one came up and gave me a big hug, and whispered Den, Den I replied.
Suzy took over and told them to sit down and put on their seat belts. She also had brought me a present a little carry out paper bag, consisting of a fresh coffee and a cheeseburger with fries.

Suzy asked could she put the destination into Doris?
I replied feel free and as Suzy touched the controls and quickly entered the coordinates, Doris beeped loudly twice then expressed a statement, "Re-enter your direction again, there is trouble ahead." Together with a visual warning the little display screen was flashing bright orange with jet black writing.

I have not experienced a Satellite Nav system say anything like that, I was puzzled
Looking at Suzy; she showed no sign of worry for her it was a normal reaction.
Doris had always kept me safe and if she says I keep guard. We drove for a couple of hours, I was thinking I fancied something to eat, and a fresh brew. Now I am sure that I didn't convert my thoughts into words, Suzy remarked that was a good idea she too fancied a coffee or something tasty.
Another popular decision agreed by the two whipper snappers, I spied a little cook café ahead, how we ended up in the café was a mystery, I don't remember turning off the main road but we munched through the lunch time menu, and they had a children's special that day. Paper hats, face painting and inflated balloons and discount vouchers for the very next family meal at their chain of restaurants.

Suzy was still feeling down, the kids were bouncing they had had a great time, Suzy too had enjoyed herself but in her own way. Back on the road again, heading for my workshop and see what was waiting for me, then get Suzy's car repaired and her back on track.
Around twenty minutes from home, Suzy asked can I talk with you in confidence?
Of course, you can.
The girls were playing in the back of the van I kept seeing balloons floating around, then an occasional scary painted face looking at me through the rear-view mirror.

That little person could be chased away with a quick verbal Boo. Then squeaky voices reading aloud a story from their new story book they got at the last meal stop.

Suzy now settled in herself, started, I have been very silly, and because of this foolishness, I have lost nearly all my insurance payment from my deceased husband, the accident that he was involved.

OK, tell me, Doris indicated at least twenty minutes before destination, she went on to say that Jim her husband had worked in the garage that we were at today, he used to take large cars over to the continent for some big wig in the town.

I never knew who it was behind the business.

Ok, I knew of similar business trips that other trade's do similar trips, most of them are quite honest, however there are exceptions.

This last trip he made, he was taking an expensive car over to Brussels and bringing back a motorhome that had been loaned to some client of the big wig, and some goods were supposed to be on board.

I think it was drink or cigarettes or something like that anyway, on the way home, there was a crash, he was killed the vehicle was a total wreck, then I was told it caught fire destroying all the goods being carried inside, it was a total write off.

We had discussed the chance of going over to Brussels and starting a new business, his trade was a precision engineer, he specialised in the aerospace technology, but the absolute finer details, I know he had with him over 50 thousand pounds that had gone missing, then I was contacted by the company, Higgott Clump & Spigot, initially then something happened to that company and Hardy Abel & Sangster declared that they had taken over the now bankrupted Higgott's law business saying that they were working with the same insurance company that was handling Jim's claim as well as other claims, and they could make sure that the insurance company paid out the insurance claim quickly.

But she had been asked to see the partner Sangster and he said he would take personal charge of this case, if I was willing to help him.

I replied without going any further did it involve a bedroom and sex?

Yes. Suzy replied, but it was a lurid office top desk.

she went on to tell me more than I really wanted to know.

From what I had heard, I reckon she was duped by this guy Sangster who caused the whole problem, possibly causing the entire problem.

Can I think on this, and call you, as I would need to find out some more information?

Sure, Suzy replied she looked a lot brighter now.

We were just pulling into the yard, and low and behold the fucking brake pedal went to the floor the main brake had failed, I managed to stop the van using the gearbox and hand brake. I am glad Suzy had chatted with me on the last twenty minutes, I had slowed the drive to a minimum I wanted to hear her story, this vehicle is going to have the worst inspection of its life, every nut and bolt panel and crevice will be torn apart and checked, from one end to another.

There were too many problems and faults for this vehicle to have, resulting from an accident.

I showed Suzy my flat, saying I consider this place safer than that motorhome; treat it as your home until I can get your car working.

Ok.

Entering the garage carrying the replacement drive shaft, Suzy's car was still on the lift, simply sliding one end into front stub axial and then fitting the flexi joint a few nuts and bolts tightened the job was finished. oil level in gearbox had been checked, back axle checked and ok, Les and I had bled the brake system earlier, while we had the car on the lift, we checked the disk pads all were in good serviceable condition.

Just to check we put the car on the brake testing machine and all met the levels required for that car.

Les enquired why all this work on the brakes?

That motorhome lost its brakes, as I drove into the yard today, the first day out, it nearly killed the children with a carbon monoxide build up in the inside lounge area at the race track, the air vents were blocked, it would have killed us at the race track had we slept in it overnight.

I am worried that there is a connection with Suzy that motorhome and the death of her husband.

I am making sure that when this car goes from here it will not cause a problem to her at all. With that I got into the car and even took it for a good test run. I returned the car was a basic car but it drove perfectly well.

Parking her car in front of my flat; I told Suzy that her chariot, is waiting to take her anywhere.

She was happy with the news and sad that she would be leaving, how much do I owe you?

Mmmm, I held my chin between thumb and forefinger, as if in deep thought, then the little one ran up to me and held my hand, that threw me, stopping my leg pull.

How about the cost of cleaning a motorhome.

By the way that bill has already been paid so this account is already settled.

Wow! I received the best three hugs I have ever had.

I think you ladies now have credit with this garage. Let me know when you get home, and if everything is ok all repairs to your car are warranted for one month.

I gave her one of my cards. I helped her carry and pack her property into the car.

A quick wave as she left the yard. The job was finished and a satisfied customer life can't get better than that.

It was a nice feeling when you see the full of damaged vehicles, but an even nicer one as the yard is cleared.

My happy but stressful day was at an end, calling in the office, to see who was covering the night shift; the brothers thought it was me, as I was freshly revived after a weekend away, with a new female in a posh mobile bedroom.

Yes, get a life I replied. Oh; by the way do not drive that motorhome or use it. It is dangerous, ok the brothers understood my dilemma

Just Three Lads

Ok I am off to bed see you lot in the morning. It was good to slip into my bed knowing the only thing that would wake me was the telephone.

During the call of nature woke me, I walked past the window where I could see the yard a moving light beam from underneath the motorhome, now who would want to be under a motorhome in my yard.

Unless it was midnight scrappers cutting off the catalytic converts, a recent spate of that had just started or someone else up to no good.

I was on my own and the element of surprise may persuade the burglar to go away, however I was inquisitive, I wanted to know who it was, what they were after, then if there are recriminations you know whose door to knock on.

I put on some work clothes went to the flat intercom and pressed the button three times, this was an already know signal to the other brothers we had an intruder in the yard.

Silently, I entered the yard, and walking quietly up to the motorhome keeping a road wheel in between me, and the light, I managed to get up to van side, and saw a foot sticking out from the vehicle.

I thought now what do I do, pull him out or jump on his foot and fracture his ankle, then at hand on the back of the little wrecker truck was a coil of light rope, the lift arms, were already about seven feet up.

I slipped the rope in a hangman's style noose, over his ankle and pulled the rope tight then threw a loop of rope over the lift arm, whatever he doing under the van was taking some effort. I went back to the wrecker truck pulling the rope as I went the rope tightened and I could

feel him squirming on the rope. I had already hooked the other end to the winch and had started to reel him in
The arms lifted the rope tightened.
Brilliant, move, I had caught one.

What a whopper, he was dragged clear kicking, and trying to get free, not a word was spoken by him.
Moving the lifting beams higher until his arms were a few inches clear of the ground then I stopped.

Well, well, well, I said what type of fish are you, or are you a snake in the grass or do I know you?
Not wanting to get near him until I recognised him, could he have any mates with him, I decided to make sure, I jumped into the wrecker truck and drove it to the middle of the yard in front of the garage doors. The automatic lights switched on the yard now bathing by the powerful floodlights displayed the whole scene.
I telephoned Les, as he answered,
"Yard now, don't Piss about, we have something on a rope?"
Now what or whoever I had, was squirming a bit.
Are you going to say hello, or be ignorant and hope you're going to get away with it. Too late sunshine here is big bro.
Les came running up and stopped to admire my catch.
Was it a long tow job?
No just minimum charge from the motorhome to centre of the yard, well, there is £100.00, and an evening call charge.

Just Three Lads

Les said £125.00 must be correct in these matters don't forget the Vat. and he is lucky it is not raining. As there may have been a wet weather charge.

You know our guest hasn't had the decency to say, Hello, or a good morning, not even a grunt.

He is keeping his balaclava gear on, and he still has a pry bar in his hand so he is in a dangerous specimen.

Les saying should we call the police and had his telephone in his hand ready to call.

'No, they would only come arrest him he would then say that we tied him up put a balaclava on his head and we would be in the wrong.

We still never find out who he is.

We could wash him to make sure he is clean and leave him hanging out to dry.

Now there is an idea.

Kevin attracted by the commotion in the yard came running still in his pyjamas.

The pry bar whistle past my ear and then clattered to the ground behind me, I picked it up and looking at it, this guy's got quality gear this is made by Slap-On tools. I laid it back down where it landed, now he has one more claw.

Kevin said "Where is that?"

"Though his belt loops a smaller pry-bar that could be a problem'.

Nope I don't think so, throwing a steel bar at your bro is an act of violence.

Kevin started up the high-pressure washing hose pulled the trigger and the machine whirred into action,

make sure the water is on I said, I would hate to see him only get a light wash.

Just Three Lads

Still no sound from the figure hanging on the rope
Kevin gave the waist area around the other pry bar was
hidden. a good washing still nothing he tried again a bit
closer.
Nope he was still hanging on to it.

Plan B

I stood next to the washer and pressed the heater button,
now the machine started to rattle and rumble as the
heater turned the cold water into steam, and high-
pressure steam. good enough to shift the most stubborn
mark on any surface.
One waft across the body area and water now turned to
boiling steam was starting to through a muffled cry
sounding like bastard came back, the pry-bar was
dropped on the ground, but still close enough for him to
grab if he had a mind to it.
Les pressed the button on the steam hose, the blast of
scalding water and steam has tremendous power this sent
the pry bar spinning away across the concrete yard.
Then a hand wrench clattered to the ground, that too was
dispatched to the yard corner.
Now what do we do with him, fist lets have this
balaclava off.
It's your choice mate, you pull it off, or we blast it off,
Kevin doesn't care.
You are on our land, and attempting to steal, our goods,
and you could have fallen by accident into the oil pit
over in the corner as you leapt over the wall.

Just Three Lads

It would take ages to find anything that went in that well, we use the oil for our own heating, so nobody empties it but us.

Ok, ok, I give up came the cry, the balaclava was pulled off.

Mr John Wade. Now; long time no see, now just how long is it since I saw you last.

It must be all of five years before yesterday, now it will be twenty-two hours since, you fixed my motorhome, and let me fill my tank at your expensive diesel pump. then my brakes failed as I was driving home, had I not been listening to a story, I may have been driving faster and lost my brakes on the Motorway, now that would have been very dangerous, I may have been killed.

I was fuming, Kevin sensed my fury with this Berk, called out "De-wax the bastard's ears,"

Les punched the big red button, A stream of high-pressure steam restarted as the internal boiler was getting the pressure up.

Les turned the dial for a two-inch fan on the spray, "You get a better job when the spray cleans the crap away." The pulsating spray was about an inch of his head when Wade screamed out you won't do it you haven't got the guts,

Kevinn walked up to the plate and took the steam lance from Les "If they don't, I have."

now if you start at his boots, always start at the top and the crap runs to the bottom and is easier to wash off, Kevin gave his ankle a cursory fan over the target area.

then John Wade screamed "ok I will tell you what I am after." I held my hand up let's be hearing it then, get me down from this first, Kevin hit the button the truck arms lowered, and the once bold defiant Mr Wade crumpled to the ground, Kevin and Les helped him to his feet, and then looped the rope around both his hands and lifted him up until his feet just touched the ground.

I have seen this on TV, Kevin said, they can't get off.

'I am waiting for this story, enough pissing around' John Wade started. Many years ago, a rich client called Mr Clump wanted a car bringing in from Germany, and converting from left hand to right hand drive, simple job I thought and quoted him a price, car arrived and the parts were second hand but nearly new, then he got one of the lads to go over and pick up a car and we did the conversions, we had quite a good thing going, it was steady work for a year or so, then he started getting crashed cars and straight cars,' 'Ringing them?' I remarked.

'Yes, sort of' John Wade continued,

'Then he was taking over one car, and bringing back another on a regular basis, funny they both had the same registration number, then he progressed onto commercial vans under the three-ton mark, they for some reason came through on the same track as the cars.

Mr Clump then tried a few motorhomes, sending people over acting as families and returning a week later with that actual van or with another van.

It was getting complex; my place was getting like kings' cross station with the comings and goings.

I commented, 'Why the interest in this motorhome'? That one was the one that never returned from a trip.

The driver died after an accident.

"So, what were they carrying"?

Just Three Lads

I don't know, after the crash they came to your place and removed some of the cargo, some of the cargo was left and they would retrieve it as the salvage would come to me; then when they went back to pick up the salvage, in your yard, it was burnt down to the chassis, they took one look and fled.

That was the end of it, until you appeared in a similar van and the client saw the van in my place.

I was about to empty the hidden compartments when you came back.

Well, you did not find it did you, because that one came from the far side of the country, yours was burnt out after Kevin made a mistake when he was cutting a damaged part off the chassis with the cutting torch.

So, piss off and tell your pet client to get stuffed, and which one was it Hardy Abel or Sangster? "Sangst-" Wade Stopping abruptly, Wade didn't finish the name.

'Thank you got it now. Good-bye Mr John Wade I take it you don't want this mentioned to the Police?

Kevin dropped him on the floor and unravelled him from the rope, and frog marched him off the premises.

Kevin moved the wrecker truck, as the truck moved away laid underneath a wallet, inside was £200 in cash, a couple of business cards in the name of John Wade and his Garage, a credit card. Plus, other trivial papers.

I thought, I will place that in my desk draw, just in case he reported it stolen, then he blamed it on me.

I could say I had been burgled; the wallet was found at the scene of the crime. If not claimed over a period it would be destined to the coffee fund.

Just Three Lads

Chapter 9

Sitting down to a morning coffee, the three of us were chatting and laughing over the capture of our villainous intruder, and showing the error of his ways.

Les remarked "He got it wrong with the motorhome didn't he. I loved your quick remark about the burnt out one, how was he to know we had just dragged it in.

Kevin you will have to more careful with the gas axe".

"Bollox to him, he shouldn't meddle in our garage, we don't meddle in his, what's dragged in by us stays with us, Kevin grunted. I was amazed it was nearly a joined-up sentence making sense.

I spotted a young lady in a mini skirt leaving Les's flat, "Is that one of yours Les"?

Oh yes, he stood up and waved her good bye "calling out to her are you coming back tonight"?

She made a sign of she would call him on the telephone walking briskly out of the yard.

I replied "A big girl, and a bonny girl, I am impressed.

"Now, listen up, I remarked, I would like to have that motorhome over the pits, and let's find out exactly what was hidden in those secret compartments.

Kevin, let us make sure we don't leave any damage I want to sell it on.

Kevin, remarked to help look in the nooks and crannies, we could try his new device. Returning from his tool cabinet he caried an inspection camera, this will look up, before Kevin could continue Les jumped in with "Your backside"

"How crude" Anyway, we look and if anything is found shout out however trivial. Ok, we all agreed, the van was hoisted by the wheel free lift, this type of lift, enables you to walk round and inspect the vehicles underside without restrictions.
Now Wade said he had already emptied the diesel tank, and all he found was a pair of knickers, and a plastic bag.

Kevin dropped the wheels, and the spare, then he removed the tyres, so he could inspect inside the tyre, if nothing found refit the tyres balance the wheels. As we were removing parts and inspecting them, we made a clear area next to the van for the inspected parts.

We found some marks from Wade's pry-irons in the dirt on the chassis gave us an indication where he was looking.
Using Kevin's endoscope camera, it was brilliant we could see into welded sections and they were all clean.

Whatever was hidden in this van it certainly wasn't in the bottom, but John Wade had two pry bars and a 15mm wrench. We continued looking, Kevin noticed a leak in the brake pipe near the back axle, he called me to let me see the weep, then just putting a couple of spanners on the joint, it was neither tight nor slack, but a weep that over a period would empty a brake master cylinder,
Kevin nipped the joint tight again. In fact, I went over every brake pipe joint and double checked the tightness of the joints, all were tight and in good order. We scavenged the entire chassis section and found nothing,

so the wheels were refitted and set the motorhome back on its wheels.

Motorhome interiors and soft furnishings are a pain, clean hands and coveralls are the order of the day when working on interiors, laying clean stuff out in a workshop however clean you keep it that grimy finger print or black mark always appears Kevin always wanted to wear the vinyl coveralls, he managed to get some from a couple of accident scenes, in where the police forensic detectives use them to keep crime scenes clean, he found a couple of sets of white, blue and one set in pink.

Kevin chose the pink, nothing was said but eye contact was made between Les and myself, Les and Kevin pulled out a new tarpaulin, spreading it on the ground, we were ready. Within 30 minutes all the cushions, and seats were removed, the cushions all had their covers removed.

Under the front seat covers another pair of knickers was found, and a brassier, all the ladies' underwear was zipped inside the cushions covers.

The draw where we had put other ladies' items was emptied and the panties and brassier kept clear from other stuff. all the draws were extracted turned over and placed on the tarp, the sliding draws inspected inside and out, nothing was found, out came the cooker also the fridge there was nothing found.

We sat, and looked at the van interior, it was bare there was nothing left "You know, when we repaired the van none of the internal panels were removed, nor any of the seats, just the area around the driver and where the screen was broken, the sun visor was replaced, I wonder, looking at the wall panels one looked slightly out of place. I pointed at the panel.

'What you reckon guys? it's Just got to be removed, it is the easiest one, to look, all the rest need lots of stuff removed to get at, Les remarked, you seen the piles of stuff on the tarpaulin, looking back, good grief what a pile. Returning to the wall panel, Les was unscrewing the top rail, remarked these cross-head screws are worn out, new cross heads are usually used once, regular removal bruises the edges of the cross, these have been used regularly, showing me one as it came loose, you could see the bruising of the incorrect sized cross head screwdriver being used on them.

as the panel was removed, the cladding and insulation was sandwiched with a paper lining from roof to floor, the paper edges disappeared behind adjacent panels on both sides of the interior, well let's see just how far this finishing paper goes.

why wait said Kevin and flipped open his blade knife, he made a small slit and ran the blade from the top to the bottom in one cut, a brown padded envelope slipped out, Kevin caught it, "It's just gave birth"

"Use your knife again, no point making a mess, Kevin slit the package open revealing its contents, it was stuffed with sealed packets of £50 notes.

"This, is a good game, finders' keepers then, Kevin inquired.

Les had taken off the other two top covers, and then eased the panels, to enable him to see behind, peeking he stated 'this backing paper goes halfway into the panels, and is taped onto the other paper cover.'

He eased the panels away from the outer metal panel. And found a loop of tape, pulling on it easily pulled clear to reveal lots of bags taped up against the wall.

Les looking at all the other panels said none of the panels had been removed the screw heads are still full of dust and unmarked, so unless we want to remove all the panels and risk not getting them back again, it is our decision.

Kevin remarked how about that probe thing would that not show what is behind. We could try drilling a hole and see. let's try then, Kevin shot off returning with his prize possession a lithium battery powered micro drill, he looked at the panels, found a place that would be covered by a seat cushion, or similar panel he drilled his little hole, and then inserted the probe, taking great delight in emitting "oohs" and "mmm", lifting our hopes and then saying "Nothing here chaps,", and moving onto the next panel.

I think we have all the hidden packages we unpacked the packages and sitting them to one side. "What do we use cladding "? Les asked Kevin remarked, we have a roll left over from the flats when we did the roof insulation last year, I will get it, and disappeared again coming back with a large roll of yellow fibreglass padding.

Measuring the cavity Kevin was amazing he laid out the fibreglass roll on the floor outside, and then cut out the section placing it into the hole, it was impressive.

He seemed skilled in this type of work. It took him 20 minutes to fill the holes, as he was doing the last hole, he remarked, 'Hello, who do you belong to. He prised out a gold ring, and passed it to me, a gold ring with a pattern, bit like an eternity ring, and it was engraved inside "from me to you."

Now that is a pretty item, that could give someone load of awkward questions, if they asked for it back?

Satisfied we had not found anything else; we started the reassemble. Then placed the fridge and the cooker back into place making sure they gas joints and the exhaust tubes were sealed and safely attached and the air vents completely clear of all obstructions. All the carpets and cushions, were put back in place the cabin looked well groomed, and untouched by human hand, including Kevin's.

So, what did we have left?

Fifty envelopes of cash money, an unknown amount.

Two pairs of knickers sized medium (three if you take the pair in the fuel tank)

1 brassier sized 38 dd

Various ladies' appliances strictly for enjoyment purposes. A gold ring. Kevin said, we have no cuddly toy.

A horn blew from the gateway, we also stopping our investigations, with us being engrossed in the search; we had not opened the gates today.

"Let's put this lot where the sun doesn't shine,

Kevin said he would organise that. His large hands grabbing the bags of cash then filled a couple of bin liner sacks he took them to his flat, and stashed them in his secret place, under his bed.

Les opened the gates and a moment later Suzy drove in.

She looked lovely, a lot brighter than the previous day, she was dressed in a black miniskirt, a dark purple cashmere sweater and her perfume was intoxicating, and was better than what our office smelt of.

She was carrying a small parcel with her; she laid it on the car bonnet and said that is for you guys with a special thank you from me and the girls.

Les opened the box looked inside, with one of those on the premises it's time for tea. Then headed off in the direction the office canteen, really it wasn't a canteen more like the shelf above the fridge and kettle.

What have you brought?

looking in the box it was a large Carrot cake.

How did she know that was our favourite, within ten minutes, we all had tea and cake in our hands happily munching away?

Suzy had said that she had a telephone call from the accountant Hardy Abel and Sangster, and they were withholding the payment of the cheque until I sign the release receipt. I banked the cheque before I got the telephone call, and I am not sure what to do.

How much was the cheque for, £3250.00?

How much were you expecting, at least similar figure but with the decimal point two points to the right £325,000.00.

Wow. That is an interesting amount. Just then Charles our solicitor walked through the door, looked round and spouted, "Morning Chaps got a spot of trouble with the old banger; it isn't doing what it's intended to do. Can you chaps have a look and hit it with the magic stick"?

Hi Charles, any idea what area we need to look, yes, he said, its chugging like a tractor.

It's, a Volvo, it is a tractor, Les exclaimed.

Just Three Lads

Let me have the keys I will look now a few hours I should have it done.

Now have you, got thirty minutes to have a word with this delightful lady and see if you can help her with a problem, I think she is being taken to the cleaners by a member of your profession. Oh, he claimed, we cannot have that.

Can I use your office need privacy and all that.

"Ok Suzy, Charles may be a wee bit odd ball, but he is really good, let him have a look at what you have got".

Suzy gave me a funny look; do I really have to show him. What,

Sorry, I meant explain the problem; you have with the solicitors handling your husband's case. I will look at his car while you have your meeting. One Volvo estate wagon in general terrible condition; we have kept this thing running for years, he should have changed it ages ago, but if he gets from A to B without passing go, he is on a winner. Lifting the bonnet, the first thing I saw was a spark plug lead, it was hanging loosely and not connected to the front plug, putting the plug lead back in place the engine resumed normal working. Oil spillage on the top of the rocker box, some sloppy person had put some oil in it and spilt it down the engine, the bend in the dipstick indicated the cause, if it was pulled out clumsily, and it could have pulled the lead off.

Checking the oil level, it was ok, then bending the oil dipstick straight, then replacing it in the hole in the side of the engine block.

I noticed his brake fluid level was halfway down the reservoir, quickly I looked at his brake disks, they were corroded and disk pads required very soon. I will tell him when he is finished with Suzy.

Parking Charles's Volvo outside, I went back into the main office. Sticking my head through the door, "Is it safe to enter, I enquired.

"Yes of course all done how's the motor"?

"Bent dipstick" I replied,

Charles replied "No need to be cheeky,"

I replied "No, it really was a bent dipstick, when you filled it with oil the dipstick it pulled the spark plug lead off, not guilty Milord, it was a petrol station attendant; I was getting blinded in one eye with that orange light on the dashboard, Charles chortled back.

'The one, with the picture of an oil can on it?

"Yes, that's it a damn bright light."

"I am glad it worked" I replied.

"Everything ok with Suzy, I enquired

"NO! This lady has a serious problem!

And with a bunch of excellent vagabonds, lowlifes and terrible representatives of the legal profession."

"Can you do anything?"

"I will need lots of proof and what I have, just isn't enough, they have a track record in these cases, how they get the work is a mystery.

Charles had changed his jovial voice tone, to a serious, one I had never heard before.

"OK Charles, your carriage is fixed and ready to take you to destinations afar, however you will need brakes replaced and within say 1000 miles.

I have reset the trip meter."

Charles sniggered "I have a trip meter wow, where is it?"

That row of numbers that goes round when you drive.

When it reaches 999 be prepared to bring it to us and get the brakes done, or maybe a new car?

"What, never, a new car, disgusting idea, screeched Charles

"How much lolly, for what you have done, it is the same as what you charged Suzy for the meeting,"

"How do you value a slice of Carrot cake Charles Replied?

"You mean you scoffed the last piece."

"Sorry, old Bean, I must dash,

Charles the whirlwind jumped into his car and disappeared out of the yard leaving a small cloud of blue smoke where he had been parked.

Thinking to myself one day that vehicle will just expire with Charles in a pile of smouldering paperwork. Suzy in hysterics with laughing; "I have never seen anything like that before, you two had an unbelievable rapport."

"Good isn't he. is one of my favourite customers, and a good Solicitor, I concluded.

Chapter 10

How do you fancy, lunch with me, if will be expensive,
and a select clientele, its Syd's Place round the corner.
Suzy asked, "Do you, eat there?
Well, we consume food there, not sure about the eating
Are you ever serious,
"Not really, you just get worry lines"
Ok, I will accept your lunch invitation. Let's go eat.
Informing the other brothers, "Going for lunch at Syd's,
we walked out of the garage, turned left, and left again
into Syd's Place
The menu was hanging from a huge nail sticking out of
the wall.
Syd's special and chips
Syd's Plaice and chips
Syd's Fish and chips
Syd's Sausage and chips
Syd's Pie and chips
Syd's chips and chips
Syd's bread and butter
Syd's sweets
Syd's pie and custard
Syd's pie no custard
Syd's custard.
Syd's tea
Syd's coffee.
Council watter
"HI Fanny, how things? Take a seat; be with you in a
minute.
Where Is Syd Suzy is asked "Oh Syd died".

"What off?" "Syds Special."
I got one of those looks again, when a woman doesn't believe you, I pointed to a table in the window.
From this table one could see anyone going into the yard, also what was going on in the café.
Fanny appeared and asking, what did our darling heart's desire, what is the special today.
"Steak and Ale pie, chips, peas and bread and butter, and for dessert Bread and butter pudding and custard is optional.
"I would like fish and chips",
Fanny enquired, "Cod or haddock"?
"Cod, if possible
Sorry haven't had Cod, for a long time",
"Will Haddock or plaice do?".
"Haddock will do nicely",
It was nice and fresh this morning.
I ordered two haddock lunches. Fanny returned and prepared the table, laying out a clean printed paper covering, then laying out a table setting equal to or better than some uptown restaurants, Fanny whispered I have some good quality white wine, I found it excellent, with the fish",
"Yes, Suzy accepted a glass," then, gave me a large wink as she spoke.
The wine was served in chilled wine glasses, the fish followed shortly.
Suzy was a bit fearful about what was coming, but when the meals arrived, she was overwhelmed they were perfect, even the chips were hand cut and stacked in a tower of six, lightly browned and irregular cut, the fish had a light dusting of bread crumbs and cooked lightly

with a slice of lemon and a small portion of fresh garden peas, and even on a lovely bone China plate, the plates did not match but that didn't matter, the meal was the star and it was delicious, even I felt I could polish off a second serving.

Suzy tucked into her meal then cleaned off the plate with the bread. "I must say that is one of the best meal's I have had in ages.

"Not bad is it." Fanny has worked hard to keep it going after Syd died, she never really liked the greasy spoon image and the decision was made to tidy it up to a bistro style. the food inspectors were happy with the modifications, she also managed to acquire new but good clientele.

The evening dinner menu is brilliant if you're not booked you don't get in, but I always manage to get a seat somewhere sometimes it is in the kitchen with Fanny and her chef.

Over one of Fannies excellent coffee's we discussed what Charles had advised.

Suzy explaining in precise detail, Charles has come across these guys before, he said he would love to blood Sangster's nose with this case but without substantial and irrefutable evidence, he would not take it to court. It is rumoured, they may have a couple of judges in their pockets. Thus, they have immunity in unexpected quarters.

Sounds like a set of upmarket thieves and the bigger they are the bigger the fiddle.

Suzy groan quietly, the state of my finances is dire, I will have to vacate my home if I don't get a job, and her hand went to her forehead, I don't normally have a problem or talk about such things but after Jim died all things went haywire.

What was Jim doing?

He was driving cars over to Belgium, and bring back other cars some were for repair, he would do a couple trips a week, the pay was very good.

and then a few years ago he did a trip with a motorhome, he would take out a motorhome and bring back a car, and then take out a car, and bring back a motorhome.

I hated it especially when he did the motorhome run.

Why?

Because, she went with him; she was always there when Jim travelled out, but never when he came back.

Who is she?

A woman connected with the guy who ran or owned the business, I never really knew who she was, he kept a lot of that side of the business quiet.

When did this happen?

Twenty months ago,

They were taking a motorhome to Belgium; Jim was also going over to look over a precision engineering workshop that was for sale.

He had completed the Belgian trip and was on his way back from the ferry, when the accident happened.

Where was the accident, just down the road from here on the old road, Jim drove into a lay-by, and evidently into the back of a parked wagon it was carrying some metal thing that was sticking out the back.

That thing crashed into the front of the vehicle and killed my Jim who was driving. The driver of the wagon ran away, but turned himself in the next day claiming he had broken down and just managed to get the truck off the road into the lay-by.

The police also said they found evidence of another passenger in the motorhome, but Jim was found alone. I didn't know until a week later.

The Police came round the house to ask me another question, they maintained they had discussed this matter with me previously, but I am adamant they had not.

For some reason, I could not make them understand that.

I saw the officer write down; on a statement I was in shock due to loss of my husband.

"Who was the insurance company"?

"Not sure but I have the details in my car.

I will let you see it later if you wish",

"Ah that would be nice",

"What about the paperwork"?

"That as well, if you really want to".

I could have said that is the best offer, I have had for months, and if it was offered, I certainly would not refuse.

Thinking about it and talking about it is two different matters. thinking best to keep quiet, with my reply.

"Let's go back, the other guys may want a lunch break",

Settling the bill, I complimented, Fanny for yet another excellent meal, and compliments to the chef.

We left and walked back to the yard. Les met us as we turned the corner, I was just coming to get you, just had a call, there is a massive pileup on the northern slip road, they want two vehicles,

Well send two,

we have no attendants for the second one,
call Nobby down the road see if he will stand in?
Kevin was already dialling knobby, a few well timed
grunts, Kevin replied he would pick up Nobby on the
way, and Les would go with John who was the other part
time mechanic.

The big wrecker truck sprang into action and both
vehicles powered off down the road with all their orange
lights Flashing.

Ok, Suzy, I can see I need a temp for this afternoon, if
you like I will pay you, £10 an hour for the rest of the
time you are here.

Suzy's eyes glistened and she immediately accepted the
position, what do I do? Boss.

Depending on how big this accident is depending on the
news media attention, however, we will be busy with
paperwork and telephone calls from the newspapers for
the rest of the day.

Giving Suzy some instructions, we are about to be very
busy, it will happen within the next hour.

If anyone calls, with concerns about today's big
accident.

We have no details, nor do we give any information over
the telephone, the police will give nothing out until after
the wrecks are sorted.

If anyone asks for me on the telephone, and if they want
me, I am busy with a client.

However, if you can ask their name and repeat the name,
I will be listening, then I will nod my head, if I want to
speak with them, or shake my head for a no.

Suzy quickly understood, and she took control of the
telephone, outer office, and the reception desk.

Just Three Lads

The mobile phone rang it was Les, he was coming back with a bad one, and could I make sure the garage was open, as this one had to go under cover immediately.

Suzy conveyed the message to me. I opened the main doors and moved the motorhome to the far side of the yard where it normally is parked.

Walking back, I noticed the short pry-bar still laid where it had landed, I picked it up, and walked back towards the office. The new tarpaulin was still laid out on the garage floor, if Les was bringing in a bad one, we might need to cover it straight over, away from snooping eyes.

Les swung into the yard with a large car on tow; he reversed it into the open garage door as he dropped it to the floor, we both pulled the tarp over the vehicle.

Fatality?

No, the driver walked away from it, he was panicking about it being crashed and demanded it be put in secure covered storage.

Les, now free of the first car, went back out to get another one.

Kevin arrived with the second of many to come, this one was a frontal impact, the car's bonnet doubled over and crumpled up to the screen, radiator was dripping fluid and possible engine oil.

Fatality?

No, the driver was shaken up a bit and was taken to the hospital.

Park it over against the far wall and throw a catch tray under the engine to catch any leaking fluids.

If there are any bad ones that need covering let's have them in the garage under a tarpaulin, as they walked back their Trucks.

Kevin and Nobby dropped the car then shot off back out to get another one.

All went quiet for a while.

Back in the office, the telephone was ringing non-stop, Suzy was coping well under the strain, shielding me from calls.

Then she answered a call, her eyes went wide, she wouldn't say the name, covering the handset, it is Mr Sangster we evidently have one of his cars.

I took the call,

"Hello I am sorry I cannot give out any information on vehicles we have here",

"But, But Do you know who I am",

Sorry Sir you could be God almighty but now until I have police clearance, nobody gets any information we are sorry and good day, then I just put the telephone down.

He rang again and demanded to speak to the owner, I said, when you get through can you tell me how you did it because he died six months ago.

Then put the phone down again. I felt a hand on my shoulder.

I loved that, it was excellent way to tell a prick where to go, and a lovely way to put somebody down, then she kissed me on the side of the cheek.

The telephone rang it was the police accident control room, I have some details for you, just one minute Suzy replied, explaining it's the police with accident details, I pointed towards a book box of forms with P.A.S. printed down the front, the forms are in there and self-explanatory.

She started on her first form, and explained back to the operator, she had just started and this was her first car to be booked in, the controller was sympathetic and she helped Suzy with any items she was unsure of.

Suzy and the operator chatted away and pages of the car's details were given, both Les and Kevin were back in the yard moving and parking cars up, then going straight back out for the remaining cars.

Suzy checked through the car registrations and said it's not here.

What is not here?

Sangster's car, no listing of a vehicle with his registration. she had already been out checking, the front registration plate was on the list, she even had gone to the rear the impact had must have broken the plate and it wasn't to be seen.

I then went out and checked the chassis registration plate, these are always visible through the bottom righthand edge of the windscreen, and duly made a note of it.

I did a couple of checks, on the computer and it would appear we have a concealed stolen car here.

As this man Sangster was such a nasty piece of work, and very exact in what he did, I did not want to be caught wanting. I thought, to cover my backside and true to the client, Mr Sangster might had been sold a spurious vehicle, I would happily check for him, I placed a call to a Detective Sergeant Harper, I knew in the stolen vehicles squad, informing him of the car we had in and the owner who was a solicitor or accountant that was going crackers to get it back.

Harper enquired Oh, please, tell me more.

I gave them the serial number and the registration number on the vehicle, and where it was picked up from. Ok we will attend to it.

Please impound it. Magic word rental just increased; ok it is impounded until you release it.

Phone calls from people and families wanting to know about their vehicles and drivers, most of them wanting to tell us their version of the accident and how it was the big black car that caused the accident.

This is getting more interesting. Additional calls from Mr Sangster demanding to know where his car was.

Yes Mr Sangster, I was talking with earlier, I switched on the telephone conversation recording machine at the same time, how may I help you.

I believe that you recovered my car today from an accident on the dual carriageway this afternoon.

I wish to come down and remove some important papers from the boot.

Ok I replied and do you have the registration number of this vehicle,

Yes, he replied giving me the registration number.

I have just received the list from the police; I will check it now whilst you are on the telephone.

Checking through the list, I replied very ceremonially, I do not have that registration on any vehicle under our control.

Well what vehicles do you have.

I am truly sorry but I cannot give you that type of information which is a matter between insurance companies and the vehicles respective owners.

Is there anything else we can help you with today?

Just Three Lads

The telephone went dead.

"Such a nice telephone manner" I remarked then switched off the answer phone, rethinking he is going to call again, I switched it to automatic, there was a smell of fish here and it wasn't our past dinner.

Suzy was answering her mobile, I heard her say I have a part time job and will be home soon.

I waited for her to inform me who it was, she looked and said it was the two girls, they had arrived home from school and were going round to my elder sister for their tea, and no need to rush home.

"You mean there are two of you"?

"Yes and no, the first yes, we are twins, "identical"? No but very similar. "One has a mole and one hasn't".

What a teasing question, I was busting a gut to ask, where is the mole?

And before you ask, I am not telling she said with a cheeky grin.

But there is a third sister, and that is the one they are going too. She lives around the corner from me. she was my sister-in-law; she has two girls the same age as my two and that is the sister they are going too.

I cried "I give up",

"I hope you don't, I was just starting to like you and of course the challenge.

My twin sister, I have not seen her for years and as far as I know hasn't got any children.

Kevin walked in saying "We have a new face in the office",

"Yes, meet Suzy she is our saviour in our hour of mess and undress".

Kevin enquired, "Does she make good tea,

"You can ask but if you get a smack in the mouth, it is your own fault".
"Ok I will make my own",
"I will have one and me too" smiled Suzy.
Kevin departed mumbling "mugged again".

A chap appeared at the door and presented his card to Suzy
"You may have a car I am concerned with"?
"Oh, just one moment, I will get him for you.
He asked, "Who is him,
"I don't know yet; I just started at dinner time and haven't had time to ask"
He started laughing as he was shown through to meet him. It was DS Harper from SVS, I showed him the car in question, the mystery crashed job, the tarp was pulled away from the vehicle, Harpers sidekick started recording details and taking photographs with the bonnet up mor photographs were taken of the engine, then the bulkhead where the chassis number was stamped also pictures of the interior and the damage on the boot lid, they tried to open the boot lid but it stuck fast.
Where is the serial number I asked, the one in the boot is behind the right-hand rear back light. I gripped the rear light cluster lenses and pulled; it moved but it sprung back into place, I have a solution, just wait a minute retrieving the mini pry bar, then attempted the light removal again this time it released.
A series of numbers were recorded and photographed. Ds Harper made note and the rear lenses was put back in place, there is another serial number underneath the car, if we could get to see it, the wheel free lift was clear and

with some difficulty we managed to get the vehicle back onto the lift, and raise the car so we could see in, the number was partial obscured by the floor pan moving forward but with a camera the picture revealed the number, that is brilliant all three are different.

I will have to call the manufacture for this one, in the meantime this goes nowhere do you have secure locked storage, in here any good or prefer somewhere else, prefer safer if you have it, I don't want the vehicle touched, we have a twenty-foot container over in the corner, we could slide it in there, and padlock it will be under the cameras and floodlight all night, if you wish.

Let it be done. Calling Kevin can we have this vehicle in the container and lock it up.

Kevin jumping aboard a fork lift truck with extended lifting forks lifted the car and transported it to the front of the container, Nobby holding the door open as the car was manoeuvred into the container, however he could not put the car all the way in, it had snagged on something at the front, to get the last foot or so inside, so dropping the car on the floor, Kevin gave the back of the car a shove with the fork ends, it held firm for a moment, then succumbed the car moved into the container. Unfortunately, one of the forks managed to pierce the boot outer skin but as it was already damaged, I don't think anyone would be worried. Two stout padlocks on both the door opening levers. That container is secure.

Kevin took off over the yard and started to tidy up the damaged cars aligning them into an order.

I always liked a tidy orderly yard.

Just Three Lads

An independent mobile, jack the lad type of insurance estimator arrived, discussed his business with Suzy, she recorded who he was and accepted his business card, and she logged him into the yard in the daily diary, then showed him to the cars he needed to see, and started on his inspection, in his estimation all were a total loss. he finished his paperwork, bade Suzy a farewell and went on his way.

Suzy was amazed just how cars with minimal damage were to be scrapped, also telling me she would have one of those if they were cheap.

Which one do you think will be cheap and how much do you think it will sell for?

I really don't know Suzy exclaimed, "If you find the value of the car the insurance company will sell off the car at different levels, and categories, what they fetch at auction depends on the vehicle market value, unless it is fired and then it goes for a set price.

Oh, my goodness it is complicated

Well dearest lady you have been a godsend for me today it is time, how may I repay you?

What we agreed the hourly rate will be fantastic.

How about a proposition?

"OK let me hear what is on offer" Suzy sat in front of me and leant forward towards me.

We today, have been incredibly busy; the way the business is changing we need someone else in the office on admin and the paperwork, that workload alone has got steadily heavier and complex.

The Lads are happy in what they do but I feel they are not happy with paperwork. The proposition could be discussed over dinner, but I know you have two teenage devils that need keeping and tending to, and I don't even know where you live.

I could be asking you to drive a hundred miles to get to work.

Suzy smiled "Well not a hundred miles more like four hundred yards,"

"No way"

Yes way, Suzy giggled, two, no three turns I live a couple of streets down behind the yard, in those Dutch shaped houses, at the end of the road, next to dingle dell?

"Next to Dingle Dell"

But it is not as nice as it used to be, sighed Suzy.

Suzy enquired as to what memories I had from Dingle Dell?

Not telling.

OK thirty hours at £10 per hour.

Any Perks? Suzy's piercing green eyes looked into mine?

I made a note to memoir, never to look a woman in the eyes when negotiating, one flutter of eye lids and the smile and that was it.

Ok benefits are lunch at Syd's place if you like, there is an option, you could supply sandwiches for me instead?

A six weeks trial and then you may have had enough of us and wish to leave.

But that will be your decision.

"I will take it," Suzy replied.

"Now I must go and I will see you eight thirty in the morning".

I replied "just Perfect".

Suzy did a little curtsy said thank you for the compliment, blew me a kiss and left the office.

Suddenly, the office was quiet it was normal for us but after today it was strange, was it a lull before the storm.

Closing the gates on my way past, I noticed from the corner of my eye a movement, but as I turned there was nothing, yet it looked like a woman walking across the yard. Scanning around the yard nobody was to be seen.

I headed for my flat, it was feet up time, I would need a quick shower to wash away the grime of the day.

As I passed the yard sensor switch, I made sure the warning light was on then the flood lights would act automatically if anything walked, or crawled into the sensor's that criss-crossed the yard, then surveillance cameras would record the event.

It was one of the best investments we ever made. In the early days neighbours and strangers would enter at any time thinking it was scrap yard and at any hour to steal parts.

We caught a regular chap who stole so many parts from cars, then had the front to complain to the police when Kevin caught him and gave him a fat nose.

That body is now resting at taking a year or so off as we caught him on the fourth time trying to set fire to a couple of cars. He now resides at Her Majesties pleasure in jail.

Towelling myself after my shower, I watch part of the TV news, showing the scene of the traffic chaos caused by the accident, I could see our trucks towing away the cars and one more truck parked on the side of the road, painted in similar colours to ours but no identifying lettering on the side, it looked if we may have a pirate wrecker following us or scanning the police radio traffic, I made a mental note to ask the lads about this crew in the morning. Slipping into bed and closed my eyes, a slight noise, turning towards the direction where the noise seemed to originate, I met the gaze of the vision face to face, again she placed fingers on my lips and saying thank you for your kindness.

Again, I sensed a feeling of cool bare skin on the back of my hand. But this time all my senses were alert, I could not define the touch of the finger to my lips, nor the touch of her lips on mine, but the touch on the back of my hand was definite, not warm nor cold just the soft texture, as the vision leant forward this pressure was applied, then as suddenly as it appeared this vision faded against the bedroom wall, a brick bedroom wall, on the other side of the that wall was parked the motorhome.

Wide awake again I went over the feeling the voice and the face and fell asleep as before with a tormented mind

Chapter 11

I slept so sound through the night, but I was shattered in the morning, taking some strong black coffee and a dry toast for breakfast, I sauntered around the yard taking note of what was there, as I walked past the motorhome a figure was standing in the front cabin area, it gave me quite a shock. Quickening my pace to a slow run I headed towards the motorhome noticing the side door was now ajar, cautiously pulling it open then I looked inside.

The front cabin area was empty entering the interior the rear section was empty also.

Sitting down in the passenger seat, I sat quietly for a moment to see if anything else was moving around.

Not a damn thing, no creaks or anything, then an urge for me to speak.

"What kindness have I done for you, for you to thank me in such a way?" A few more moments passed, and I repeated the sentence again, but slightly higher tone.

Nothing, then a car horn blew outside the gate.

Closing the RV side door making sure it was closed, I peeked through the gate, it was the lovely Suzy waiting to get in.

Opening the large gates and securing them against the wall. We were open for business.

The bold Suzy dressed in a denim skirt, a cream blouse and high heels walked with intention towards the office door, her short stride making her chest bounce as she approached the office.

Just Three Lads

Suzy greeted me with a beaming smile, whispered "Good Morning" she looked at her desk briefly, then went and made sure the kettle was on and warming the water, ready for whatever hot brew would be required, then returned to her desk checked the paperwork.
She sorted and returned some files to the filing cabinet, and declared herself ready to take on anything.
Kevin Nobby and Les walked into the office, Kevin heading for the small kitchen to make the coffee, remarking, "Thank you to whoever boiled the kettle"
He appeared shortly with fists gripping 5 cups of coffee, and place them on the desk.
What do we have today?
I declared, the motorhome has a ghost, last night it appeared in my flat, Kevin spat his coffee across the room, don't joke about those thing's bro, he cried.
I am not joking, the vision is a female, Nobby and Les stood closer to the window to make sure they had a good view of the motorhome, asking do we have a set time when she appears?
"Stop messing around lads" cried Kevin, I looked at him he had tears streaming down his cheeks,
"Hey bro what is wrong, I never thought that you were feared of ghosts?"
"I don't know but that woman thing you're on about has been in my flat doing what you said, to me!!"
"When was this bro"?
"Tuesday night", twice during the night what does it mean bro?
"I don't know Kevin; I just don't know"

Just Three Lads

Suzy speaking softly Terry experienced her at the race track when you were sleeping in the motorhome, and you thought it was me?"
Les head turned round with a quizzical look, asked "You were naked in the motorhome with Bro?"

"NO, I wasn't, it was the ghost" Suzy replied

Les turning round, "ok the first sighting of this "vision" was at the race track on Sunday evening"
The second was? He gesturing for feedback
"Anybody for Monday?" Monday, we had problem with the motorhome and my girls got affected with carbon monoxide gas at the Race Track. Suzy added.
"Tuesday Anything?" Les enquired
"Twice in my flat" Kevin voiced again
"We took the whole thing apart looking for problems and What did we find," said Kevin
"All those packets" said Kevin,
"Where did you hide them,
Kevin replied, I hid them where the Sun don't shine"
I replied for fucks ache were,
"Under me bed, Bro sun doesn't shine there"
Kevin was happy with his reply.
"And, and," he went on to say "she was in the bedroom that night"
I hid under the bedclothes and didn't see her again. "And she was there again last night"
"Ok guys go and get the bags of stuff we took from the Motorhome Kevin go with Les in case she is hovering around c'mon Kevin,"
Les cried "Naked you say, let me see this nakedness".

"Nobby can help the insurance assessor that is just about to walk through the door, by the way no access allowed in the containers ok."

"OK boss" Nobby picking up a clipboard with the list of cars we had recovered, he met with the assessor, then pointing an arm towards the cars in request, they were at the back of the yard, then both walked off together to deal with his enquiry.

Suzy looked at me, "You never said you found anything." I never gave it a thought, we so very busy that day and even you experienced it.

By the way, just love your office uniform.

"Thank you" she smiled and took off the denim Jacket to reveal a well filled tea shirt.

"Nice" I whispered under my breath. Kevin and Les arrived back carrying the black sacks, back of my office please with them.

I didn't want Nobby to see what we discovered,

What about? Les nodded head towards Suzy

"She will be ok" I replied.

Then split a bag, let's find out what we have in there

Kevin cut open a sack, fished out a yellow-coloured padded envelope, opening one he saw, bundles of £50 notes and lots of them, ok let's see emptying them one by one on the desk there were approx. £30,000 per envelope.

Taking a rough estimate, there is the same amount in each envelope there is Approximate £1.6 million in those bags. I picked up each envelope and felt the contents, they all felt the same making a count of 55 envelopes used as insulation between the van wall and the inner panel.

now that is upmarket insulation in anybody's language. One packet was left it was a different size, slitting the top open it was crammed full of 500-euro notes so in the final packet was 300,000 Euros.

Said Kevin "Let me see"? I passed the packet to him; he started wafting himself with the money the packet split dumping its contents on the floor.

"You daft Bugger pick them up; Suzy do we have any large envelopes around A-four or A-three size?"
Suzy re-appeared and placed some large envelopes on the desk. She took a good look at the pile of envelopes; she didn't utter a word and went back to the reception desk. Kevin repacking the Euro notes into a new envelope,
Les picked up a small envelope from the floor and threw it on the desk, this must have dropped from the packet. I slit open the letter, a handwritten note slipped out, "well I can't read this it is a language I have never seen before." "Anything left in that sack"? Les looked and said "not",
"I think there is Les having another look", he plunged his hand into the bag and fished out the gold ring,
"That what I wanted to see Bro.
"So, to sum it up, we have £1.6 million in £50 notes €300,000 in 500€ notes, A gold eternity ring, then an envelope with a letter written in an unknown hand, and possible a language giving what appeared numbers, and explanations, and directions.
Not a bad haul, but why did this motorhome not get claimed before we acquired it?

there certainly was activity round the van taking out everything they could.

"If you remember we put the motorhome in the garage, as we pulled that other burnt-out shell of a motorhome in and parked it in the same place"

Les surmised "When they came back, they saw the burnt-out wreck and thought it was their motorhome, then not wishing to be identified further, buggered off without asking, thus writing off, whatever was left, I would have loved to be a fly, on the wall when that discussion happened".

Chapter 12

Stolen vehicles D.S. Harper arrived, Suzy came to tell me of his arrival, quickly opening the wall safe and deposited the pile of envelopes out of sight. The rest I slid into the top draw of my desk.

Ok Suzy let us see what this man has to say, a coffee for him as well if you please, Suzy showing him into the office, asking him how he liked his coffee, DS Harper took a seat and started with what he had found. Kevin not really interested excused himself and decided to go somewhere else, Les listened to the history of what had been found from the numbers the car had revealed, we have three cars rebuilt in to one vehicle, all the three cars are also on the road, with the same identity.

We have traced all the cars and have stolen vehicles checking the cars now. "Grief this is brilliant where are the other cars?" "One of them is owned by Sangster and we have met him, but the other one is on the south coast." Harper replied we want to have a good look at this car and see what happened to it, do you want us to do it here or back at your HQ workshop?

Back at HQ we need it to be officially checked and videoed as we do it.

when do you want it?

Harper replied "We will send one of the police flatbed pickups this afternoon and then we take it from there."

"OK by me it will be ready to go"

Now here is something new for you, and I told him about the strange going on's we have discovered with the motorhome since we moved it. I omitted to say about what was discovered inside the van.

Ok he took details of the registration document and chassis and engine number I will check this out and give you a call.

Walking out into the yard I told Kevin about the car going back to police Workshops for a close inspection, and get it out of the container ready for it to go, opening the door there was a smell of petrol from within the container, I looked underneath and saw fuel dripping from the petrol tank of the car, Nobby hooking a chain to the back of the car we slowly dragged the car out of the container, whatever snagged the car on the way in, to the container snagged it again on the way out, Kevin had to put more power on revved up the forklift gave an almighty pull and the car shot out of the container and a small fire had started inside the container Kevin acting quickly dragged the car away from the flames, there was nothing to burn in the container so we let it burn itself out.

Disconnecting the chains Kevin's heavy pull had pulled the crumpled rear end out and the jammed boot lid had sprung open.

fearing a further fire, I looked in and saw a box of files and other paperwork, Kevin and I quickly stored them in the back of the company van.

Nothing else was left in the car, then police transporter arrived and said he had been sent to get the car that DS Harper talked about this morning.

I pointed at the car that is it just pulled it from the container for you, Kevin pulled out of the way and the police driver loaded up the car onto the flatbed truck. He gave us the paperwork to sign and I gave him his receipt and he continued his way.

Back to the office Suzy on the telephone Police control room on the phone they had two to pick up from the southern dual carriageway,

ok calling Kevin and Nobby off you go, two for you.

Going back to my office I sat down and glanced over a few papers Suzy had dropped on my desk.

A fresh coffee was also in place on my desk, and then a pair of hands took hold of my shoulders, and gave them a massage, now that is lovely it thought I could do with one of every morning, the neck massage eased my neck tension and I closed my eyes surmising over the morning's activity, "Knickers Bra and Sex implements" I said quietly to myself.

Ok Boss, where do I get them, is this normal on the first day at work, do I have to bring them or are they supplied by the management"?

"Err, Pardon, what did you say?" I murmured,

Suzy sat down and said to me "Are you in trouble with your sex life"?

"No," I replied "I don't have a sex life."

Suzy replied, it was Just what you said about knickers bra and the sex toys."

Yes, I see what you mean, and had a little laugh, I was surmising, what was missing from the black sacks.

Suzy grinning remarked "I don't understand",

Just Three Lads

These items, were found in the motorhome, when we stripped out the inside, and then we got busy, Kevin put them all in a bag and hid them away.

and then when he brought them back, those items were missing, from the black sack.

I will ask Kevin when he comes back.

Suzy, can you speak or read any languages,

"Nope" she replied apart from "good and bad versions". "Why"?

We have a couple of letters written in a foreign language, Suzy beamed back the girls can, they read most European languages they are brilliant.

They learnt from a young age, all the countries we lived in when Jim was alive the girls speak and read all of them, the all ways get good results in school exams.

they have been known to tell the teacher's off when they get it wrong. Can you get them to call in after school, take a squint at these letters.

Suzy sent one of the girls a text, then got an instant reply, they would come after school?

Now what else do we have on the agenda, by the way it is dinner time.

Just as the words left her lips Kevin and Nobby drove into the yard dragging two more damaged cars both were lined up against the already growing line of damaged cars. Nobby came back in the office, one more to come Boss, it is bad one medic in attendance I will go out with Kevin and get it.

Les stuck his head in the office "Off to Sid's place do you want anything bringing back"?

"Not today for me" I replied "neither for me" replied Suzy "I brought lunch with me". I decided to make myself a coffee, "Would madam like a coffee with her sandwich"? "I would kind sir" was the reply

Now I like coffee a little stronger than the norm, asking Suzy she liked a similar style, she agreed. Bringing back two coffees, laid out on Suzy's desk was a plate full of freshly made sandwiches, Can I interest sir with something on this plate holding the plate towards me and her breasts were just pressed onto the back of the plate.

Anything I like on that plate?

Yes, anything you like,

Ok, I will have a Ham and Cheese, or I may get a smack round the chops.

What do you mean, Suzy replied,

What else is on the plate?

She looked down realising part of her anatomy was on the plate.

She started to snigger, then laughed then an, oh, oh dear that hurts, she held her side from laughing so much.

They are for afters she replied, widening her eyes as she replied

"Afters, nice one". I was laughing now.

Les walked back into the office

"What is the joke then"?

"We were laughing about fruit"

The puzzled look on Suzy faces and looking at me she mouthed "Fruit"?

"Yes, a nice Pear in the hand"

Well, I thought Suzy was going to explode,

Les looking puzzled looked at us then went into the workshop to get on with some work, what are you going to do about the mess you made on your tea shirt, Suzy looking saw the coffee stain on her top and said I will have to go home and change.

ok I said, she went out to her car and I heard a starter motor turning slowly, she had a flat battery, I lifted the bonnet and the fan belt was just about split into shreds, asking Les could he sort the belt problem and charge the battery on Suzy's car.

Let me see if I have a tea shirt that may do, the company had some a few years back.

Calling Les where did the old tea shirts go to?

"You had them in your apartment I think I saw them in the box room",

walking over to my rooms I searched the box room and found a couple still bagged one in an army green and one in pink. No wonder these did not go in these colours. Giving them to Suzy, I don't know the sizes, she would try them and find out, they are a little big she replied, and tried the pink one on, this is tight, she replied and wouldn't turn round, then she tried the green one that was a little bigger, she gave a twirl hey I remarked "Looking good",

I spoke. It is a bit big but that is better than it being too tight. "I like tight"

Kevin arrived back with Nobby towing a mess on the back of the truck; I waved him straight to the back of the garage mentioned cover it over.

Kevin came back and filled the collection paperwork he said he was not feeling well, and was going to lie down.

"Before you go; where did the other bits discovered in the motorhome go"?

"What's them bro"? The knickers and the bra! Not forgetting that collection of toys?

"Oh, them, they are still in the flat, I can bring them down when I come back. Kevin was grumbling to himself as he walked out of the office.

Suzy asked "Is Kevin ok.

Why I asked",

Probably the knickers are too tight for him, and he hasn't got the bra adjusted to fit him correctly"? She replied

Well, I was amazed saying "You don't think he was wearing them now do you"?

"Women notice things men don't"

"But how"?

"The shoulder straps were showing under his shirt" What has happened to Bro I exclaimed?

"He needs a woman" Suzy replied

Oh, dear I thought of the creature about to be released on the female population.

There is a woman for everyone, it just takes time for them to find each other.

The Girls came running into the office laughing and happy about something from school Suzy explained to the girls what the problem was and what they had to do.

I gave them the letters, as one started translating Suzy jotted down what they were saying it was a letter to a manager of a bank in one of the no questions countries to and requesting that the following funds be put into the following accounts listing how much was to go into each account.

Alas no names were included just numbers for the accounts to be opened and specific amounts to be deposited into the account, not realising the gravity of the paper, we bundled it back with the rest of the paperwork. Thanking the girls for their help I gave them

Just Three Lads

£10 each for their hard work, they were delighted and begged mum to take them shopping.
"Good bye enjoy your shopping" I waved them on their way Les remarked "she is nice isn't she"?
She is so lively, and she ticks the boxes and fits in, all problems just disappear.
I thought for tonight I would take a shower have a couple of glasses of beer relax then watch some TV until bedtime.

Then the phone rang picking it up, I listened two pickup trucks required on the northern dual carriageway, I replied leaving now ETA 10minuts from now minutes unless there are traffic jams if so, can you arrange a clear passage through the traffic.
It was the bad section we seem to get a lot of wrecks from that location.
Just, Les and I were left in the yard, we stood in and took the challenge to clear the road as fast as we can.
Two hours later we arrived back, the Thunderstorm that came from nowhere, made life just that unbearable. We had two more wrecks in the yard, the trucks in their own parking places pointing out of the yard, ready to go to the next emergency, for us two; bed after finishing the paperwork.

Chapter 13

Waking five minutes before the morning 7am alarm call.
I slowly surveyed my bedroom, a place to sleep, it was a
man pit; my man pit, and today is when Alice is due.
Alice is our housekeeper she comes and cleans; washes
do the ironing and generally mucks out the three flats
keeping the brothers respectable.
Otherwise, we would end up three hermits living in a not
so tidy cave. We appreciated visits, when she had
finished, we had fresh clean clothes together with a
respectable space to bring somebody back if we wanted
too,
The odd lady did appear with the brothers, brother Les
always had a couple of girls around somewhere, Kevin
was still waiting, what for I don't know.
My love life was none existent, there had been an odd
lady in the past, unfortunately they were as described
odd. I knew there was a hopeful female watching from
one of the parts suppliers, maybe I should ask her out
and see how things turn out. and then recently Suzy.
Suzy seemed to have taken a shine, but five days is not a
long time, but she was lovely, and although desperate,
she needed a job, was she being nice for being nice sake,
or was there some other ulterior motive behind her rapid
acceptance of friendship.
Her girls were lovely a perfect example of a steady nice
home life usually a reflection of their mother and father
influence.
The father, what happened with the father, how was he
killed? Trying to remember what Suzy had said, she had

said that he was killed delivering a motorhome with another woman, in the van by something coming through the windscreen.

My brain flashed a huge WHAT IF, it was my motorhome, with what we had found inside the van, virtually constituted smuggling and currency was the contraband.

My brain was now collating information, what was smuggled out, what was smuggled back in its place.

I was not liking the answers, having this knowledge, and not passing it on was in away aiding and abetting.

This could mean a serious prison term, the worst scenario could be the loss of the business, would be a total disaster and not of our own making.

Making a mental note to call SVS and have a chat with DS Harper, the bedside alarm clock burst into a warm melody tune much better than a harsh bell or buzzer, pressing the button to cease the noise I turned over and went to sleep, I slept for another hour.

Slowly I was woken by a female voice humming a tune, I could hear it pottering around in the kitchen. I was wondering could this be the ghostly image coming to see me again, this time I would be ready, to observe and take in all details and would try to physically take hold of her and define the apparition.

The vision appeared and looked deeply at me, good grief it was terrible closeup, and then the vision opened her mouth and spoke.

"Are you getting up or do I strip the bed with you in it"?
"Morning Alice".

Just Three Lads

"Morning, I have the kettle on, and there is a lady waiting to get in the office?
"Shit, shit, Suzy was early.
Nope I was late, I had slept in, Bugger". leaping from the bed there was another scream,
"Yoohoo, a naked man" cried Alice, as she laughed.
From bedroom to door in 2 seconds, with tea shirt on and trying to pull my jeans up on the move caused me to stumble trip and fall, I had nothing to stop me, I crashed into the floor sliding across the wood floor into the bedroom wall.
I felt, as well as heard the sickening crunch.
I remember saying to myself that was a silly thing to do, then darkness, nothing but darkness. for some reason I sensed being in a strange grey blue light. also, I was viewing the scene as if I was one floor up from above the ceiling. Yet there was no ceiling just an endless darkening darkness, I looked around trying to see what had happened, I saw a group of people fussing round a body laid on the ground, they lifted the body placing it on the bed, covering the partially dressed body with a blanket, after a while another person with large back pack appeared, looked at the body on the bed looking in its eyes, then mouth, then examining the side of the head, then feeling the body, up and down the arms, the hips, the legs, the turning back to the examination of the head and neck. The man in charge of the body was holding something to the upper chest, then the most violent pain came to me, I felt dizzy and shook my head, again the pain, I felt a surge being dragged back, then the violent shock pulled me again, I lost consciousness, I felt a warm glow and the light was so bright it hurt my eyes,

Just Three Lads

I felt a stabbing pain in my arm and neck and side of skull, I felt as if I was falling down and down a very large black tube, other people were also in this tube falling as well, some were sitting cross legged as if waiting for someone.

Then a voice spoke.

"Hello, I didn't expect to see you here."

Turning to the direction of the voice the vision of the woman I had seen in the motorhome and my bedroom was there, she was within arm's reach, I put out my arm to touch her and I saw my arm pass through her arm. I pulled back, saying, "We are all like this here, then leaning forward, placed her finger on my lips and said again thank you for being so kind"

Who, are you, I asked Looking at the vision, she had a familiar look; she had two earrings in one ear lobe and one in the other. "I am not the one you need to talk too" and waved her hand towards a dark-haired man sat cross legged, I noticed the tip of the index finger was missing, the whiteness of her hand against the darkness made the deformed hand distinctive. The dark-haired man turned he smiled and spoke." Thank you for being so kind",

"What kindness have I done?"

"You are helping" replied the man

"Whom am I helping"?

"You know who you are helping; say sorry to her for not coming back" the cross-legged man replied.

Please tell her sorry, and tell her James T knows who did this it is him.

they made it happen, they and She did it."

Then the strangest feeling of coldness I have ever felt hurt my brain and the light were getting brighter and brighter, distant voices were mumbling, in the background getting quieter until there was silence.

The peace was beautiful, I was warm and comfortable, I tried to sit up. I could not move, I tried to move, my arms they were by my side, I opened my eyes, the light made me close my eyes, I cried out, that hurts; what happened? "You should put your trousers on before you run" a familiar voice spoke; another voice spoke this one much softer tone; she placed such a soft hand on my forehead and you gave us a shock."

Why what happened, well as Alice told me she had said that I was waiting outside the office, you leapt from the bed and ran for the door pulling on your trousers you tripped and went head long into the wall and knocked yourself out.

"How long was I unconscious"? I enquired

"No more than five minutes" the soft voice replied.

It seemed that I was away for hours, I met the lady I met Jimmy, I met, I met I could not remember, it was a haze, he said I am sorry for not coming, it is him and her, they made it happen. I heard a gasp and a cry. I opened my eyes and I was laid in my bed, looking round I saw Alice, Suzy, and Les, then a chap dressed in Green with Paramedic blazed across his chest, he looked at me and spoke,

"Good morning". As he continued inspect me, he wrapped something around my upper arm, then what ever it was tightened and he held a stethoscope on my arm, then gave setting to another person by the door he then tested my heart and looked into my eyes with a small bright light, then satisfied started to pack his equipment away.

How are you feeling, he asked and be careful touching your forehead, you have taken quite a knock. To your head.

I felt my head and discovered a bandage covering the top of my head, looking round. I saw Les, Suzy was holding her hand to her mouth, and Alice was rubbing her cleaning cloth round the furniture mumbling

"don't mind me"

"Hang on, just hang on" I said just what has happened "I would like to know please".

The paramedic sat on the edge of the bed, proceeded to explain, you tripped as you were going for the door, and crashed into the wall knocking yourself out.

We received the emergency call and found these ladies had put you back into bed, you did slip away and we had to resuscitate your heart.

Confusion jumbling my mind.

I Slipped away where, where did I go?

"That's what the pain was, thinking back three times?

You did it three times

"No Sir, we zapped you twice your heart started again after the second application".

"But very interesting to hear that you remember, what else did you remember"?

"I was watching you from up there" pointing towards the ceiling from up there.

a voice from the back of the room, "Oh yes it had to be where I had not dusted yet."

Alice was getting upset she wanted to get on.

"Can I get up"?

"Yes, but it is a day off for you today,
I must insist on that. The paramedic concluded
"I will look after him; he won't get away with anything".
Suzy voiced her suggestion.
Les suggested to Alice to leave my room for the time being, and continue with the other two rooms, Bro is confused and he is getting confused.

Les approved we will take care of the business office, I mentioned to Les, if SVS, DS Harper appears I want to see him urgently.
"Ok, I will send him over".
Then Les walked off towards the office.
Suzy looked at me and now you have a day off and you must stay in bed.
What would you like to do?
I would like to stay in bed all day and have sex many times.
A voice from the other room started to laugh. "Just been dead and brought back to life and all he wants is sex… that's my boy"!!
I whispered "she has hearing like a shit house rat."
"I heard that" Alice replied, it is you that is in the shit, now,
Alice chuckled.
Suzy looked at me and said "You wouldn't be able to stand the strain".
"Well, I thought if I lay on my back and supplied what was needed, I could see how long I could last".
The voice from the other room spoke again, "Well you had better have a good breakfast if you're going for a world championship attempt".

Just Three Lads

I called back, "Can you suggest what breakfast I should have for this historic attempt"?
"Scrambled egg beans and 4 sausages", was the reply, "That's what my Mr gets when he wants to have a go.
"Is he successful" I replied
"No, he always needs a hand to finish… Oh My God. what have I just said?
Not saying any more going to do Leslie's flat now see you in two weeks. I heard the door click shut.
Suzy was just about wetting herself with laughing, "What a card she is, so funny".
"Now is that three or four sausages"?
Suzy looking at me pensively biting her bottom lip. Whatever you think?
Let me see what you have in your kitchen as she slipped out of the room. I could hear tins being shuffled about in the back room and the sound of activity, trying to lie on my back I found my neck was painful, altering the pillows, I felt better with just the one under my head.
The mouth-watering smells were wafting in from the kitchen, and the gorgeous smell of filtered coffee was enticing my taste buds, it was the best breakfast smell I had smelt in a long time.
Suzy appeared with a steaming plate of food and placing a tray on the bed; she helped me forward and placed another pillow behind my back holding me forward making it easier for me to eat.
I could see down the front of her tee shirt, and she had a lovely cleavage, a real turn on, I could feel a stirring whether it was making me better, or randy, time would tell. The plate of food was an omelette with sausages and beans all mixed in, where is the other half I enquired,

Suzy slipping out of the room came back with the other plate, and a coffee and a tea. Tea, I enquired I thought you were a coffee girl, no I prefer tea most of the time.

Well, if a record attempt is to be made then both participants must have the same breakfast.

"Yes, well and just agreed" we both tucked in to our breakfast. A timely knock on the door came just after we had finished eating.

Suzy going and opening the door, please come in, showing DS Harper into the bedroom,

"I have some coffee to make and dishes to wash."

Harper looked at me, pointing to my bandage and then in Suzy's direction,

"Are you two an item"?

Explaining that I fell this morning cracking my head on the wall, Suzy is working for me now and is taking on being chief nurse today, looking after me today the paramedic doc ordered me to rest with sleep and relaxation.

"Good advice, now Les said you wanted to see me"?

Yes, I explained about cars coming into the yard and going out and with the last car in three parts,

I was worried about and nasty drug type substances being hidden in the cars and vans, and I thought if he had contact in the drugs squad if they would like to come over and let one of the dogs go around the yard and see if the find anything. Ok he said what has triggered this worry? Having gut reaction, I replied to his question.

We had a break in, the motorhome I picked up two years ago was the target, also the last car in we discovered was three parts could that have stuff on board.

Just Three Lads

I want to be sure in my mind. I have been having ghost sightings, I and now Kevin has seen her, I explained what I had experienced to date, then this accident I had today I think I have had an out of body experience and it was disturbing. "Ok you're worried about something lets us get the guys in and see if anything turns up". Something else lowering my voice, "Can you find out about the history of the motorhome, I knew there were fatalities in it but never, the history, also the ghostly image seems to be connected with the motorhome and the Sangster crew? "I think there may have been a connection with someone I may know". "Ok that is a good order for today's inquiry". Harper replied, "best be off and see what I can turn up".

And by the way that car that went back on the police pickup truck self-ignited and the rear end was totally burnt out, yes, we noticed it had a petrol leak when we removed it from the container, I bet Sangster is not happy, he has been calling all and sundry trying to find his car, even the chief constable has been called twice.

Harper left me, I lay back sipping my coffee it had gone cold, but I liked cold coffee. I closed my eyes feeling a bit drowsy not for long I felt somebody slide my jeans off and my socks then slip into bed with me, oh! I whispered I have a visitor, my body reported to my brain, the incredible touch of naked skin on my skin.

It is only a feeling that you can experience and not explain how it feels. A soft hand lay on my chest the feeling was enticing in fact very stimulating, then soft lips kissed mine.

Just Three Lads

"Do I open my eyes or keep them closed and wonder who it is"?

"Keeping them closed it may be interesting" came a whispered reply, the hand ran up my body and circled my nipples creating a grab with her nails the grab moved nipping and twisting my torso skin as the hand moved, a warm body snuggled into mine, it felt so good, still the relentless exploring hands covered my arms and shoulders then the legs thighs and then finally found what she sought. Her foreplay was easing together with stimulation gently pressing certain parts she brought me to a near climax and stopping before the final event, she then managed to mount me and her gyrating hips found what she wanted and pounced taking her pleasure, then relaxing then repeating the process repeatedly.

Finally, our sweating body's clung together and we both passed into the realms of sleep.

An hour or so later I woke by the movement of her hips again manipulating slowly around to ease a member into a certain position locating the entrance once located the movement turned to small pushes until the connect was made, the love making commenced without the use of hands, that was a unique approach with excellent results, Sleep took over once more, wakening again to a knock on the flat door; I arose from the bed and putting a dressing gown on proceeded to the door,

"Now then Kevin what's up"?

Les says you weren't well so I came to see if there is anything you want.

Replying Suzy is here looking after me.

"Oh, I saw her in the office, maybe I was mistaken".

"In the office"?

Just Three Lads

Who was in the bed?

"I will be down in a minute" Kevin grunted an acknowledgement and went off to the garage I went back to my bedroom there was a form in the bed pulling back the sheets it was just the way the duvet had bunched up, checking the bathroom nobody there, the flat was empty. I had problem putting on a tee shirt removing the bandage from my head I could see a cracking black eye forming around the eye and forehead. My neck was stiff at one point rolling my head round my neck seem to crunch at a certain angle, keeping rolling my head the neck creak became easier. I felt a lot better and decided to try a walk around the yard.

As I descended the stairs, I became aware of a few creaks in my joints, I seem to have developed a limp, and a creaky back.

Making my entrance into the office, a beaming smile greeted me, "Is Sir feeling better"?

"I am not sure I have creaks from all parts and a beautiful black eye forming",

"Yes, I could see that, so I went and got something for that from the chemist",

"What is that"?

"Witch hazel, sit down and I will apply to the bruise. It was very cold and stung like a wasp stinger.

"This will help the bruise and it should be reducing within a day or so".

"That will be nice",

"I will be putting it on again in a couple of hours, so don't run away".

Suzy worked well all day, I sat and watched her from my office, and checked over the storage paperwork.

Just Three Lads

Making the coffee today for Suzy she was thankful for regular hot drinks. Suzy popped her head around the door, somebody for you, a chap dressed in black combat fatigues walked into the office, "DS Harper asked me to come and let you see the dog work in a test condition"
he replied in a loud enough voice for anyone listening.
"Ok do I need to do anything for you"?
The dog will find that, he handed me a cloth bag in a plastic sealed bag, "Please hide that anywhere you like", I went and hid it in the outside toilet in the yard it had just been cleaned and the smell of disinfectant was very powerful, Alice had been there.
Ready let's see what he can do.
He is a She replied the officer.
"Oh, I am sorry let us see what she can do".
The spaniel was released and immediately ran towards the toilet, she was watching I said,
Then just as she got to the door, she turned and made a beeline for a line of parked vehicles, running round and round the cars in the line, getting to the air, she stopped sniffing the air and took off again this time in the direction of the motorhome as she got near the motorhome, she stopped and cowered down then approached the motorhome slowly, quickly turning her head to see if her handler was going to call her back,
She checked again looking at her handler, she has never acted like that before, "Go girl find" he called to her, she worked round the motorhome stopped near the air vent exit on the side cautiously sniffing the air again,
"Shall I open the door"?
"Yes, please she has a scent for something", opening the motorhome door the dog jumped in followed by her

handler, she searched all over the motorhome stopping by the panel where we found the stash of money then continued into the back and started to dig into the back seat cushions.

We pulled the cushions free and she continued back into the corner the officer lifted the seat bases and the dog was straight in and sat down. That's it whatever is in there is there, then she cowered down, squealed making a beeline towards the open-door round to the back of the van and growled and barked at the outside corner of the vehicle.

Then the nose caught wind of another trace and ran towards the works van and sat down again I limped across the yard and opened the door she leapt into the rear and started sniffing the boxes in the loading area and sat down. Her handler called her giving her reward her ball, she ran off to play with it.

Well, what have we in the boxes, I don't know we removed them from a damaged car, pulling the boxes out of the van it was paperwork a brief case and files and more files, we opened all the files and let the dog inspect them, but the case was of the great interest. The catch was locked; Kevin had come to see what the commotion was all about, with the little dog.

Give me that screw driver from your leg pocket Kevin, he passed me the driver, using the driver blade I eased the lock open, the lid flew back it to reveal paperwork and emptying it on the van floor, files and five thick packets of blotting paper landed on the van floor, the dog sat down again.

Just Three Lads

The officer called his partner from the van, bring the kit, it was a small bag of bottles, taking a sample of the blotting paper he dropped it into a solution if it turns purple someone is in trouble. Purple was the colour of the packet after it mixed with a sample,

and then we were joined by DS Harper, found anything? "Yes Sir" looks like a good haul it is soaked in the blotting paper, and there are 5 large packets.

"Who, what and when"?

Remember the black car that was rear ended and you took away, this lot was in the boot, Kevin had been pulling the vehicle out of the container the damaged front suspension snagged on the container floor, Kevin kept pulling and the petrol tank split as he cleared the container the suspension had sparked on the concrete thus causing a fire, so he kept dragged it into the centre of the yard. The boot sprung open and he lifted this lot out and put it in the van for safe keeping. "This owner has a lot of explaining to do, have you found him? I asked nope

Sangster said he had sold the car two months ago but had mislaid the paperwork. But said he will find it. They checked the rest of the contents of the box and only thing of importance was the briefcase. What do you want us to do with this lot of paperwork it should go back into the car boot then it would be good to see his reaction?

Can you lock-up the paperwork for us and I will take the briefcase and then make more enquiries. We have some small lockable containers for storage, I placed the box in there and locked the door, I offered Harper the key.

"No, you keep it if I lose it. It will be a problem to get in", "I have a copy in the safe" so if I am not in you have access ok, he took the key.

Putting on a zippy tie wrap around the handle he put it in his pocket.

The dog officer talked with DS Harper and made notes then he looked at the dog, and said have you forgotten something? The dog turned round ran across the yard to the toilet the door was ajar she went in and out in a split second carrying the package in her mouth, straight back to the office and dropped it at his feet.

The Ball was the reward and she ran around again with the ball.

What about the motorhome? Harper asked what happened there the dog handler explained the reaction of the dog and what she had found,

Ok Harper let's see if she finds it again the dog ran straight up to the van ran round it sniffed the corner again and then ran to the open door and went inside this time went to the driver's seat then the passenger seat then ran back to the back of the van stopping casually at the cushion then sniffed where she sat down but turned round lost interest in the rest of the van and went outside.

I opened the cushion zipper and pulled out the foam rubber looked in the cloth cover nothing in here and felt up the foam rubber the officer also checks it over bending and rolling in his hands, whatever it was it is not here.

Then DS Harper said "There is a ghost in this van",

"Your joking" he replied, well the dog did not like something, "Maybe the ghost didn't like the motorhome being inspected by the dog and has left".

"Ha, ha, I don't know I will tell you if she returns".
The drug squad officers packed up and departed to write up their reports. Slowly walking back into the office, Suzy looked at me and what was that all about, well it looks as if your lawyer friend may be a drug smuggler but that is confidential and between the two of us. They found drugs in the stuff we took from the boot of the car and left us with the paper work but took the briefcase with the drugs.

I have a request Suzy looking at me, would it be possible to look through that paperwork and see if anything in there relates to my case that Sangster worked on. Well, if you want to look you will have to do it today or tonight as he may come back tomorrow and take it all away,
"OK can we do it now" she replied Opening the door in the container we removed the box into my office and Suzy immediately started on the files and read the details, nothing but she was taking a mental note of what the files were and what they referred to. Why is it, it is always the last one, she opened it and her name jumped out at her. "Found it"! Suzy cried, her eyes scanning the document page after page, asking "can I keep this"?
"Yes, it is yours, he has paid you".
Putting the file box back into the container, I noticed something under the rear of the Motorhome a funny looking box, reaching down I could just grip it and pull it out from underneath. It was a cardboard box with a tin inside the outside of the box was very grubby as if it had been in the spray from a road wheel, the tin inside had a polished bronze finish with a flush fitted lid. As I was examining it DS Harper drove into the yard, walking

towards him asking, "What have you found"? "I am not sure, it was under the motorhome and I haven't opened it yet", "Oh dear it looks like an urn". "You don't think she is inside"? Harper held his hands up I wouldn't know. Well, if we open it in the middle of the yard and anything goes wrong, we are outside. Slowly prising the lid off, it was fell on the ground, quick as a flash the contents started to erupt slowly then with a scream a long green snake just grew and grew as it rocketed towards the sky. My heart missed a beat then started thumping heavily, Harper leapt back a couple of feet.

"What the hell was that", Harper asked. Then we heard from within the garage hoots of laughing, we turned to see Kevin and Les bent double laughing, you bastards are on the night shift tonight and I hope it snows.

"How can I help you before I sort these two jokers out",

"That box of paperwork, my superintendent wants it all possible evidence under our lock and key, we may be investigating this bunch Solicitors".

"Ok let's get it quickly before there are more snakes in the grass appear." Harper shaking his head over the last event, continued to load the boot of his car, and waved good bye, then headed towards the police station.

To do whatever police do in their offices.

Meanwhile back in the office Suzy was nose deep in to the file she had rescued, "Coffee" I mentioned, "I will make some" she replied "No you are busy I can make some" Two minutes a steaming mug of coffee and a tea I placed on the desk, Suzy briefly glanced up at me, then mouthing "Thank you", Then returned to her research. I felt like a spare prick at a wedding, so I thought I would do something, what, shall, I, do.

I was bored, I opened my mobile and scanned through all the messages received, no new ones, looked at the pictures, lots of crashed vehicles and crash sites, then at the end of the picture file was a picture of a door with an arrow on it, I could not remember this. It was a video not a picture, press the key to play the scene I watched as things happened a door open and then a door closed, and the box of files on the floor and one of the secretaries' dropping files from a metal storage cupboard into the box, the girl was doing something with the green file with yellow ribbon, which looked like the file Suzy was inspecting. I plugged the mobile phone into my computer then transferred the video file to the hard drive. Playing the video this time on the computer with the sound turned up I saw the scene clearer, and watched the secretary go through the rituals and a faceless suit walking in giving instruction. Suzy came into my office shaking her head, those damn solicitors have robbed me, and they have manipulated the figures so I have no recourse but to comply and sign that statement to accept the compensation money, or I won't receive a penny. Listen Suzy you know when I came to pick you up that day at Sangster's, I left my mobile video camera working in my jacket pocket in the waiting area, outside the account's office, when I went for a pee, well by some fluke my mobile recorded what was going on in the file office in. What was said and done has been recorded; the video is not perfect but watch it and see.

Playing the video again Suzy came round and stood behind me to watch the screen, Suzy asked me to turn the volume up to see if we can hear what they are talking about. Not much could be heard from the girls in the office but when the Suit walked in, "Who is that"? I enquired. "Mr Sangster" Suzy replied, as he spoke it was easy to hear his instruction, to the secretary, by the time he had given his instructions, Suzy was sitting astride my knee writing down his instructions, that bastard has just told her to take nine hundred percent off your payment and then put Vat on the bill, the greedy Sod. I think I need to have a word in his ear. So, whatever you were paid you need to add the 900% he deducted and that is the actual figure you should have got. You have the cheque and you have banked it if he stops it, he would not like this to come out in court, Suzy please don't worry about any money problems, I will see that you are not short changed in this case.

I have a couple of tricks up my sleeve. I think Charles may be interested in these findings. I will call him and explain what we have. After a deep discussion with Charles, it is still a skimpy case, with the way we obtained the information, but he wants to give it a try he will call in and look at the paperwork and video.

While Suzy was still sitting on my knee the girls called Suzy, I could overhear their requests to go and stay with their cousins and go to see the show uptown, could they go? There was plenty of please mummy, and please mummy, Suzy relenting, laid back with her head on my shoulder, saying "that's me having a quiet night, or could I interest you in pork and egg Pie and Peas and a mug of tea"? Will I have to dress for dinner? Suzy looked into my eyes replied "Would you prefer Baby doll or pyjamas"? Only joking I replied. Calling Syd's place to see if he was open tonight, yes, he said until 8.30, can you do a little meal for two with trimmings. Ok whenever you like just walk round Suzy, I just called Syd's place she can fit us in tonight for the extra special.

"Oh dear" she replied, "Can I go freshen up in your flat"?

"Of course, you can, unless you want to go home first", "I have everything I need in here" holding up a small bag, and she headed off towards the flat door. Thirty minutes later we closed the office and organised the work rotor for tonight, I am of for a meal with Suzy. Knocking on the door as I entered the apartment, I could hear singing coming from the bedroom, I stuck my head through the door calling out hi I am going to take a shower, Suzy was doing what ladies do in front of mirrors. Stripping off, I slipped into the shower, boy o boy, did that feel good; warm water on my bruises stung at first, then relenting as the skin warmed up.

A quick sponge over then a good towelling down, finishing off with a shave, that was best of all the skin feeling clean again. Walking back to the bed room I took some clean Y fronts, pulling them on, a quiet voice said "I am glad I wasn't looking the other way Mr.",

"Good grief, I totally forgot you were in here I am very sorry and I am feeling embarrassed now".

Well and truly caught with my trousers down, I continuing to dress a clean shirt clean slacks socks and shoes then I went to put on a dab of after shave, looking at my selection I chose one. "Don't wear that one it has bad memories for me",

"That is ok it wasn't my favourite one, but is smelt better that engine oil, will you choose please" Suzy scanned the

array of bottles and found one," I have never seen this one before",
"Looking at it, I had got it on holiday many moons ago and I liked it but then thought it a bit feminine". It has a nice aroma as she smelt the open bottle top, tipping some into her hand she liberally splashed some around the chin and rubbed her hands around my neck, then sat me down and applied more witch hazel to my bruising. The mirror reflection gave me a shock the flesh around the eye was a dark blue with the forehead was yellowing. I could put some makeup on and disguise it a bit, no leave it, it will go soon and I can't see it but I bet it looks scary. Entering Syd's place, the window seat was decked out with candles and napkins the full works. Fanny looked at me and said "What was the other guy like"?
"I don't know Suzy got me with the brick in her hand bag" "Cool answer, please have a seat".
Would you like, "Red or White"? "What have you prepared for us"? "Is venison steak ok for you"? "Yes please, and the Red,"
Suzy agreed with my choice. We got a few looks from the other diners sat at their plastic table cloths and a few looks from guys at my shiner, then thinking best not to say anything. The meal was excellent, the company was delightful and the different topic of conversation was good, work talk during the meal was a taboo subject. All too soon it was over, slipping a couple of folding notes enough to cover the bill into Fanny's hand.
Standing outside the café I asked would you like a nightcap or a tea or coffee?
"There is one thing I would like"?
"What may that be"? I enquired

"A walk and keep chatting to you, I have had a lovely day, and meal and delightful company",
Let us see how it goes I have a slight headache and would love forty winks. Down the street round the corner the old saying of taking the air, this form of exercise was good, we chatted more totally disregarded the time. I stopped and looked around; I know the area around the yard.
But I could not recognise where we had walked to,
"Do you know where we are"?
"Yes, the yard is half a mile as the crow flies in that direction. Suzy pointing an arm with an out stretched finger in a direction, and my little house is over there in that direction. Which is the shorter route, I could do with a loo..." My house two minutes come with me, walking a bit brisker saved the day. Returning to the living room, I must apologies for that, normally when you are driving you can hold it a bit better and always speed up a bit when desperate. Sitting down on the sofa Suzy came and leant on the arm, "Now would Sir like a drink on the house"? That is very decent of you "What does madam recommend"? I have tea, coffee, a dry white wine, a soft drink coke orange juice and Blackcurrant juice. Black tea with a small sugar would be welcome. Looking round the room, it was sparsely furnished but neat and tidy, a distinct lack of a television set or even a place to stand one, there was a radio and nice small music system and a small laptop computer set up on a coffee table by the wall. Suzy presenting me with my tea, and sat down beside me, "are you not having one"? "At bed time I will have a warm milky drink".

Just Three Lads

A knock on the door got Suzy to her feet quickly, I heard a gasp of surprise as she met who was there,
"What is it you want, I have company.," whoever was in the hallway spoke lots of harmful words, with replies like "No I won't do it" and get out of my life. and "I can't do it now, I am entertaining, go away."
The living room door flew open, revealing the visiting female, she strode into the centre of the room, she looked me up and down, saying "Is this all you're entertaining, did you black his eye"?
Suzy shouted "Lizzy Shut up! This is my Boss",
"Oh, I do beg your Pardon", as she spoke, she also hiccupped, giving the impression of being intoxicated.
"Take no notice of Lizzy she is drunk",
"I gathered that".
Let me introduce my sister Elizabeth, she is my twin I am ashamed to say.
Taking a second look I could see the resemblance, the clothes and dress sense did not follow between the two women, maybe if they dressed in the similar clothes, they would be identical, the eye see's what it wants to see. Lizzy sat beside me,
"Have you bedded her yet?
If not, you can have me now, I am much better"!
The look on Suzy's face was of horror, I could not believe what she was asking and didn't really want to be around to hear, what other verbal sentences, were about to spew forth.
"I am very sorry but I can't really answer that question nor would I wish too. "

Just Three Lads

Suzy, do you want this person out of your house? She doesn't want to leave, I can show her the door, or come and stay with me.

Suzy relented saying no she can stay, I will go and leave you to your company, I will see you in the morning"

Suzy showed me to the front door, her little face deep in sorrow spoke very quietly "I am extremely sorry and embarrassed about what has just happened,"

I placed my finger on her lips, "please don't worry about it, but I know you will, and I gave her a kiss and left." I thought I knew my way back and stood at the end of her garden working out which way to the office and yard. I could hear raised voices emitting from Suzy's house.

Sounds like a sister, sister relationship that isn't working... Not knowing on the right direction back, I set forth and totally got lost, returning after ten minutes to the same road end, realising I must have walked round an oval estate. Under difficult situations brain inspires actions. Pulling out my mobile phone, I selected a map and zoomed in I could see where I had gone wrong, I turned round walked past Suzy's house, the argument was still going strong, a few streets later the Yard was on my right, going into the yard a light on in the main garage.

It was Kevin looking at a car he had just brought in, a tasty German hot hatch with slight damage to the front end. "What you reckon Bro just bought off the internet auction site for a steal, needs a bit of work and it should go like stink"

"Good move, ok I'm off to bed, I am tired worn-out, and feeling shattered".

Just Three Lads

The idea of slipping into a cool bed on your own is lovely, also the feel of a warm naked body in the bed as well, then remembering the morning lovemaking flooded my memory, it seemed a dream, maybe it was.

Suzy did not mention anything about it nor made any reference to it, as if it didn't happen.

Whether happened or did not happen my mind was past caring slumber and the warming bed soon sleep controlled the next hours.

Chapter 14

I overslept, the repeated knocking on the flat door, forced me out of bed, and slowly opened, to see DS Harper, "Oh dear did I wake you? Well, it is nine thirty, and it's a terrible day outside"

"Come in Harper take a seat, I will get dressed, I was still feeling the effects of yesterday"

Harper and I chatted as I managed to pull on my jeans and a shirt not knowing whether it was clean or not.

I was having a bit of trouble focusing this morning.

Finally taking a morning constitution, then onto the living room via the kitchen made a tea and coffee, Passing Harper his tea and sitting down, to what was going to be a discussion of a fact update,"

Well Harper I am sitting comfortable you may begin."

Ds Harper started,

Item 1 the Motorhome. Prior to it being used in the last trip where it crashed, it had been on and off the continent several times, enough mind you to attract the attention of Customs and Excise, they had stopped it and did a couple of searches going in both directions, nothing was ever found, sometimes the driver would be a male and sometimes a female a couple of times they would be together. The couple were white, a light brown-haired female and a dark/black haired male. I noticed he had a picture of the woman as she was driving the vehicle and a picture or the man. Now the male was killed in the accident but the female was never found although there were two types of blood found in the motorhome at the scene of the accident. I added the family soon came to recover the effects from the motorhome the following day, Les dealt with them he had to tell them not to take all the cushions and stuff until the insurance company had seen it, they didn't seem to care, he said the insurance estimator was due that afternoon and after he had seen it, they could take what they wanted. Ok Harper making a note of that event. Then he continued "Did they come back"? "No" I replied, "I had gone out on a call out, when I had to recover a fire damaged motorhome about the same size and the yard was getting full. We had to shuffle the vehicles around to create space.

We replaced the fatality motorhome to the secured garage and then the fire damaged motorhome in its place.

There was no further contact with the family and I had no contact address, thinking I am sure that there was something amiss with the address on the recovery sheet there was no telephone contact number and I even went round the house, it was a fictitious address. I asked a couple of the neighbours either way about the motorhome none knew of such a vehicle, so after nine months storage I claimed the vehicle under the storage rules of the company, Even posted an advert in the national press to advise anyone, there wasn't a reply to that so we assumed that the fatality driver was the owner and he had no further use of it. Ok Harper replied asking a few more little bits re the motorhome, I think that is that one put to bed.

Item 2 the triple identity car. Now this is an interesting one the middle bit of the vehicle is registered to our

friend Mr Sangster. The other two parts front and rear came from other vehicle that had been scrapped and chopped up for spares, very cleverly put together, a little better than the average cut and shunt man, the middle part belongs to Mr Sangster the front and rear comes from the other two vehicles. Now the most important part was the paperwork in the back, it was destined for the incinerator, and our legal team have taken a browse through and it is a plethora of altered invoices stealing money from clients' accounts, to a value of say that box is over twenty million pounds. All very nicely done very hard to trace and account for. But we have a problem in and actual prosecution as there are no signatures or anything connecting any of the three partners to the crime, and if pressed they will as likely drop it onto a scapegoat in the office. Thinking quickly, it would be best to talk about Suzy's folder. I made up a plausible story when we were transferring the files from the car to our van, Kevin let the box fall on the ground spilling the contents out on the floor, Suzy came to his assistance then helped him put the papers back in the box, she spotted her name of the cover of one of the files, then she asked if she could read it. As I had picked her up from Sangster's office, they had been handling the case for compensation for her when her husband was killed. It bought no problem as it was information and data connected with her. I do know she was ripped off by that crew of solicitors for an incredible amount of money.
Ok,
I will have a word with her on that; I know she is seeing our company solicitor this morning about the case, even more interesting. Harper added, making more notes.

Just Three Lads

Looking out of the window into the yard in fact they are in the office both of them at the moment, do you want them over here, yes a good idea, I will go and tell them to come over when they are ready, I did my best getting from my flat across the yard to the office, briefly I informed Charles about the other files and what they have found, and to be safe, I told Harper re the file you have there as well, it may be the trigger they require, also there may be more information in the box you might need in Suzy's claim. Charles said he had a few more bits to do with Suzy this morning then they would come across. I gave Suzy a wink, and she blanked me, strange reaction, Suzy kept her mouth closed all the time, I looked at her again are you ok? She nodded. Putting this down to the strange mood's ladies have. I returned to finish off with Harper. I walked back to the flat and within half an hour the list of problems was sorted to our mutual satisfaction just leaving a few items to clarify re the accident and the paperwork Suzy had interest in. A movement in the yard distracted me from the meeting Charles and Suzy were walking to. the flats and Suzy directed Charles to the wrong front door, she went to Les's front door. Waiting whilst Suzy knocked, I opened the window, saying you would get a better response from the door under this window you're at the wrong flat. Quickly they came to the correct door, I let them in, I followed Suzy as she followed Charles up, Suzy swung her hips I bit more that she normally did, her perfume had changed also, again putting the changes down to ladies' options and choices. Charles and Harper sat in deep discussion and Suzy taking serious note of what was said, an hour passed and then another hour so much was talked about it was getting beyond me. Charles and Harper conclude that working together they may be able to get Sangster brought to book.

I made some tea for the group; serving tea all round, then unexpected Suzy claimed she didn't like tea, and only drank coffee. Puzzled I made coffee for her, and she was happy again, I said sorry about all these problems that are becoming known, and she replied well it is all my money that will be returned when it comes.

Harper concluding replied "Well that is all I need for today" he and Charles exchanged business cards, saying he would see me later. Seeing Harper to his car, "Sorry about the offhand attitude of Suzy I haven't known her long", "I wouldn't worry the minute we seem to get involved this hard shell seems to appear, it usually depicts she has something to hide."

"Ok bye for now", Taking a scan around the yard all was quiet; I could see the guys in the garage beavering away on Kevin's new toy.

Back in the flat, "Anyone fancy some lunch" Charles, Suzy, agreed that they could do, In Syd's place the menu was as ever good although Suzy ate what she had ordered she kept very quiet, Charles tucked away at the special, this is brilliant never had such tasty food. Charles let me into a secret, this case could be big and the money involved is huge, the way those guys work I cannot believe they have got away with it for such a length of time without detection. Harper will be pulling out of the investigation as it isn't his bag and a specialist accountancy detective will be making his presence felt shortly. Charles wiping his lips with the serviette, "Well that is me done, time for me to be off to the office and

crack on with the getting things correct." Now Suzy, what do we have for the rest of the afternoon, nothing in the book she replied, "The lads are busy, the weather is good so the chance of a call out is low, and what would you like to do"? "How about an afternoon in bed? Was the replied suggestion I remember me saying to myself if it was on offer, I would take up the offer. An afternoon in the sack would be delightful, "Who's place then yours or mine"? "Well," she looked with an impish grin "Your flat is closer" c'mon then let us see what mischief we can get up to in three hours, why three hours, well that is when the girls come for you, she looked a bit vague. Ok then and walked with me back to the flat. As the flat door closed the door, she turned round taking hold of my belt and plunging her hand down the front of my jeans, taking hold of me, she pulled me up the stairs towards the bedroom pushing me backwards onto the bed then clambering on top of me and adjusting my pillow, "I need you comfortable, I have been known to get a little wild." Walking to the curtains she closed them making the room darker She excused herself found the bathroom, within a minute I was about to ask are you ok, just then a naked leg appeared round the door, all that the lady was wearing was one of my ties, standing with her hands on hips, the tie hung loose around her neck down between her breasts and covered her femininity slowly walking into the room, climbing onto the bed she teased me with the tie, and dropping to her knees her legs either side of me, clumsily
undoing my belt and sliding it from the belt loops then unzipping my jeans she pulled them off. Then pulling off my socks, my shirt was ripped open the buttons flying in

all directions. Just leaving me and my modesty covered by my boxer shorts, sitting astride me she started at my mouth and then worked round my neck down my chest biting and nipping with her fingers as she proceeded down my body, this stimulation was good but slightly painful, but I would not complain and see what happened, the legs were not immune to the tantalising biting and nipping when she had finished my body glowed with a revitalisation I had never experienced before. Let me see what is causing this lump in your boxer's, slowly pulling them down from the outer edges what could snag the boxers removal was certainly working I was standing to attention, sliding them off my legs; she then sat on my stomach and started gyrating her hips, around and down until she had the tip of me in the lips of her vagina, slowly taking her pleasure she lowered herself onto me making sure I had no place to retreat to, then she sat up straight curving pushing her head back and pushing out her magnificent breasts. Slowly leaning forward, she waved the breasts over my face and lips. I opened my mouth to kiss her as my lips connected with her nipples she gasped and rammed herself hard onto me, I could feel the grinding of pubic bone to pubic bone. Shrieks of ecstasy came from her mouth as she lay back onto my raised knees; she gently continued moving her hips as if she was riding the winner in the three thirty at York.

Then she eased her exciting movements to a gentle slowing movement held on as she climaxed earlier than I managed to leave me wanting. Then she turned round mounting me again holding my ankle she began the riding movement until again she climaxed before I could. She snuggled up to me and whispered on top now please. As I moved, she repositioned herself underneath me. I lowered myself onto her body and she quickly had me held by her legs gripped me and pulled me in this time she let me ride the four thirty winner all the way home, winning in a lathered sweat. We then slept a short while, then Suzy slipped from the bed and as she walked away from me, she had a dark mark on the top of her bottom just where the cleavage of the buttocks met the small of the back. It looked like a beauty spot. Then remembering that Suzy said one twin with and one twin without, but refused to say who had what and who didn't. I heard the shower running, walked to the bathroom door, would you like some company in there, you may rub my back if you like, I didn't ask a second time I soaped up a sponge rubbing the soap onto my hands, then slowly rubbing the soap onto her back and down the cleavage of her bottom the mole spot was raised slightly and I gave special attention to her buttocks. Then taking the sponge I washed the back from top to bottom, and round the buttocks, turning her round I repeated the soaping to the front of her body I gave the front the same attention as the back, taking the shower head from the wall bracket she showered me down and washed all the parts we had used that afternoon. I retrieved clean towels from the airing cupboard and hung a towel around her shoulders and one around my waste. Then went back to the bedroom and dried myself with the towel on the bed while I was drying my legs Suzy walked back into the bedroom walking straight to me and pushed me on my back, lent over me I was about to say something when she placed a finger on my lips kissed me with her breasts pressing into mine. As she pulled away, I had a startled look on my face, what the matter you look as if you have seen a ghost! Oh Wow, I have enjoyed that that was something I have never experienced before, it was special She quickly getting dressed in front of me no shame said she must go and sort a couple of things out I watched her walk across the yard and walk straight past her car walk out of the yard, raised her hand a large black car swept up stopped by her side, she got in then the car accelerated away. Virtually at the same time my mobile telephone rang, hello its Suzy, "Yes thank you for that" She went on to say "Sorry I have not been in today, Lizzy so upset me last night. she hit me and I have a blackening eye colour like yours,"

"Oh, my word, are you ok, what happened" I enquired. Lizzy quizzed me all last night about you, and what was I doing with you, and Sangster.

Then the whole scene seems to orchestrate into a bad argument, then she hit me so hard, I fell striking my head and I didn't wake up until a few minutes ago, I tried calling you on the office phone but I got the answer phone, so I left a message.

That was the time I had gone with Charles and the other woman to Syd's Café.

"If you're sure you are ok, are the girls ok"

"Yes, they are ok they are with me," she said "Lizzy had quizzed them earlier about the weekend away and what had happened with the solicitors." "She took some of my clothes from the clothes rack as she left, I don't know why,"

Just Three Lads

"Don't go anywhere I will come round, I need to make some calls urgently, then I will come straight round."
Just before you go you said "Yes thank you for that, what did you mean"?

Oops, I could not tell her, that her twin sister had, screwed me silly all morning in my flat. also, I could not tell the difference, between them,
I was thinking about something else, and you caught me on the hop.
"Ok ",
Suzy replied "See you when you arrive."
Charles, hi it's me, now listen I have just discovered that woman at the meeting this morning was not Suzy it was her twin sister Elizabeth, Lizzy, I think she works for Sangster, I have just talked to Suzy and she is hurt and was assaulted by Lizzy last night.
What Lizzy is up to I don't know, will her being privy to the case details cause Suzy harm, "No, now I am aware of it I can alter paperwork to make sure we are in discussion with the correct twin. Not such a problem I can get sort that out, but she does have copies of the case I have against Mr Sangster, that may be compromise our position. Let me call DS Harper and tell him, Charles said let me call him the between us we can formulate a plan. I told him about the dream and the ghost image and what Lizzy had said to me as she left, it was identical I am still trying to work out the connection, I think the original woman in the motorhome at the time of the accident was Lizzy and she managed to get out although slightly injured and disappeared into countryside. I will ask Suzy if she has a picture of her husband prior to the

crash, then compare the picture DS Harper has in his file. Jumping into the company van I drove round to Suzy's house and she saw me coming and opened the door, ushering me into the lounge, the place was all smashed up, who did this? Lizzy did it last night after you had gone, then smacked me, well I can say you have a cracker of a black eye. placing a bottle onto her table, I brought you a present, the witch hazel you brought me for the bruising; I went into the kitchen even that was in a mess. tearing off a couple of sheets of kitchen roll, then liberally dowsing the paper, here hold this on your bruise passing her the soaked poultice.

I returned to the kitchen to try and make it look like it was before, five minutes after I found the kettle in the garden, washed it out and made some tea.

She was grateful have you eaten, no I could eat anything the children are with my sister-in-law, they are fine and Clarissa is happy to keep them over night until I get sorted out here.

Where does Lizzy live Suzy told me the last address she had for her, I texted the address to DS Harper, also saying she had vandalised your house and beaten you causing actual bodily harm. Within two minute a Panda car was parked outside with a couple of police woman taking charge and starting to interview Suzy, photographs were taken of the face bruising and damage to the house.

Why all this I am not pressing charges, I am your employee and this woman has interfered with one of my employees at work and gave false information at a legal meeting causing deception, and perverting the course of justice is always a good offence that is open ended and can stick.

"The other thing Lizzy can be apprehended and asked many questions, while the Police can check her story, they have a way of detaining people and crooks.

The garden had stuff littered around, finding bin bags in the cupboard I started to pick up bits that looked fresh dumped plates, saucers, cups less handles, cutlery, even bed sheets, pans, and tins of food were strewn about. Five minutes later the garden was tidy. Placing the sack in the kitchen, Suzy would have to do the inspection of the sack and keep what was good and chuck out what wasn't. The police officers had finished with their interview and only had the paperwork to write up and they departed, leaving us alone.

Chapter 15

Suzy sat with me on the sofa, she clung on my arm, she was pale and shaking her voice had a tremble in it as she started to tell me

"I think you had better tell me the story and this time the one with the woman, the Motorhome, and any connection with Sangster."

"I will try" she replied. "Jim and I managed to find work all over Europe, he was a skilled engineer and fixed anything that he was presented with, he managed to get a job as a how you would call it a, repair engineer? for a large Swiss manufacturer they made industrial gearboxes. These were used in machine manufacturing; you know the type of machinery that made factories work.

The factory was closing, the work force was dramatically reduced they only kept on Swiss employees something about labour laws and job guarantees, but it was still discrimination, whilst the factory profits were good, the smaller the wage bill and profit margin increased, and as the old story went, it all looked good on paper. Then one day Lizzy came round listened to Jim's dilemma and she said she may know of a temporary job for a while. Furthermore, it paid good money for people who can do things and were conscientious.

The job entailed moving, sealed secure documents from one office to other offices and transferring similar documents from office to office and offices on the continent.

All was going well, and then the operation changed to moving the odd car and van even wagons around and sometimes a wagon with a tractor or farm machinery on the back, those runs he did to Southern Ireland and Rotterdam.

The work was good Jim did well he managed to make all the deliveries on time and was getting increased work. He would pick up the cars and bits from that Garage that you took the motorhome to when I went to see Mr Sangster. Lizzy had a relationship with the garage owner but I am sure she was seeing Mr Sangster and one of the other partner's as well. I did not talk about the marriage bed but she was different, she would talk proudly about her recent conquests, and it made me feel terrible. She flirted with all men, as you saw yesterday, and last night after you had gone, she said that she would go and see you and tell you what I was really like if I didn't help her. Lizzy said "The motorhome you had was the one Jim was killed in, and I said it wasn't as you had told me it came from another location, and the other one that was towed in was burnt out. She said that she was going to impersonate me and took some of my clothes to affect the disguise to perfection. Well, she had me fooled, Also Charles was fooled, and she had gone through some paperwork in the office, what exactly, I don't know but I will check in the morning or later tonight.

Charles! Oh no! what did she do with him, well she is now Privy to all that you and Charles talked about the other day. "But later on, I reckoned that you were being impersonated by Lizzy"

Just Three Lads

How did you work it out"? She doesn't like tea. you drink the stuff all the time, she was turning her nose up at Sid's menu, where the three of us had lunch. Oh, she would not like the look of Syd's café. she would put up with it so she could gather the information from us.
"Do you know; I think she has been acting like a spy but for whom"? Adding more of my thoughts on the subject.

"Yes" Suzy added "She always liked spy stories and being very secretive about her work, and her type of businesses,". "When she left today, she walked from the yard past your car and got into a large black car that she hailed from the yard gate, not caring whether she was observed or not she must have got enough information she required to finish what she has started, whatever that is" I remarked. "When are the girls back"? My sister-in-law can keep them over night, I replied "no they are better off here under your control, Suzy called Clarissa and said she could take the children back now if that was not a problem, Clarissa replied they were out getting Fish and chips and she could drop them off in a minute, quickly relaying that to me I commented she could get us fish and chips, I will pay her when she drops off the kids. "They should be here soon"
"Ok that's tea sorted, what's the next problem? She looked at me and said I don't know. "Ok Madam get your backside into gear, upstairs shower and change and put a face on your going to have a fish supper."
Suzy eager to please and a fish supper is better than sat on a sofa moping, while she was upstairs, I straightened up the room to how I envisaged it, moving stuff around, I discovered a picture of Suzy and a dark-haired chap,

the content of the picture also had one of the girls a lot younger than they are now, if the other girl had taken the picture, this must have been Jim, Suzy's husband, a handsome chap.

I could see why she fell for his charms, I always envied guys with dark hair, come to think of it, why? I don't know. Taking a copy of that picture on my mobile phone, I could compare the picture with the picture that DS Harper has on record. The front door burst open two girls running in, spied me and stopped in their tracks, "where is Mum the eldest asked"?

"She is upstairs taking a shower, Clarissa also walked in took one look at me said are you the Boss man

"Yes, I replied, by the way how much do I owe you for the food? £25.00 she said lots of everything in there I was going to join you but since I am free tonight, I am off to play some Bingo with the rest of her friends, I will join them at the end of the road.

"What car does your aunty Lizzy have girls"?

"Oh, she has a red convertible one, a has a badge with SAAB or whatever make that is, that is what it says on the boot lid." you wouldn't happen to know the registration number, the little one, said yes, it is L1ZZY. I texted Ds Harper with that info it might just help.

Soon we were fed and watered, I was feeling tired and wished my bed, for me it had been a strenuous day.

The brothers were working on a new car, Suzy asking whose car was it, meaning, the one being worked on, Kevin has towed the car in, we will have to wait to see if it might come our way.

Suzy leant against me as she rubbed the top of my thigh, will I stay tonight?

Just Three Lads

Not tonight I replied I was a bit sore after the bashing I had received with Lizzy only a few hours previous, and then the girls were wittering on about their homework, and urged Suzy to help them. she agreed, then I left after a big hug and my buttocks being nicely caressed.

On the way to my flat, I popped into the garage; I told the lads I am off to my bed. As I snuggled down into the bed, I could still smell the female perfume, memories flooded back about her body her actions and whilst deep in thought sleep took me again. Waking during the night, I was sure something was happening and looked in the yard, nothing to be seen, I questioned were the flood lights working, then the light came on as the garage cat ran across the yard with another cat chasing her, satisfied the lights worked I returned to bed and drifted off again.

At four thirty the telephone shattered my slumber,

The Police control room, requesting assistance, a wagon was on a bridge had crashed, and the one of the tractors was precariously might topple onto the Motorway below. We are on our way; I had raised the lads and all three decided to attend.

I travelled with Les, and asked him had he noticed another wrecker crew shadowing our call outs?

He had and he forgot to tell me when he got home, what do you think his plan is, les wasn't sure but if he turns up to this one, you can ask him.

Chapter 16

Not sure which actual road, the incident was on, I drove down the motorway, and Kevin following. the distant blue strobe lights on the police vehicles guided us and our orange flashing lights joined the spectacle, I stopped on the approach road to the bridge, not knowing was I better on top or underneath, as decision brought a smile to my face. the fire Tenders had telescopic floodlight tower erected. Now half the motorway was closed; We walked to and surveyed the scene; one tractor was secure the other was half off the flat wagon and resting on the bridge road fence and the whole unit was parked on the front end of another car this still had people inside.

I thought Kevin and Les with the bigger truck would be better on the bridge and string a cable to the Tractor. and then drag it back into place on the flat wagon. Passing my idea on, les had the similar notion.

Les driving up the slip road and positioned his truck, Kevin pulled out the cable out assisted by the boys from the fire and crash tender. The cable secured and Kevin started to winch in the cable. The tractor started to move and luck had it rolled back into place on the flat wagon. Now the paramedic guys could get safe access to the car's occupants, those souls were jammed under the front of the Articulated tractor unit, two people trapped inside the car. the brigade guys were jacking up the Artic unit, the slight movement made the farm tractor move Kevin reacted by tightening his winch rope, thus stopping any further movement.

Just Three Lads

A straight pull on the car forward would free it from its present position, I discussed my idea of pulling the car complete with victims out from under the truck cab, the rescue workers didn't like it but something had to be done and quick.

Les quickly strung another chain onto the unsecure tractor and winching it secure again, he put another chain on for extra safety. Securing the rear of the car to my tow truck and winching the car creaked groaned then the car became free, with no damage to the people inside, pulling the car to a safer distance away from the articulated truck the truck was set down on its wheels again. It was ready to be moved.

During all this mayhem going on a very large chap with flowing blond hair and yellow tee shirt met with the Police officer overseeing the accident.

He claimed that the two tractors and the other farm implements on the truck belonged to him they had been stolen that very night from his farm just ten miles down the road.

He discovered them missing then heard about the accident on the radio, upon hearing that two tractors were on the trailer so he jumped in his car and drove to the accident just to see if they were his property.

He inspected the load and gave enough information about the machinery to prove they were his property and could he have them back. He was deep into harvesting and he needed them urgently,

"By the way where is the driver of the articulated wagon? I asked,

Now there is a funny thing the driver was nowhere to be seen, he had been sitting on the side of the bridge and had just vanished. The large chap in yellow tea shirt introduced himself as, Ian the Farmer from Pleasant farms. Chatted to me as we prepared to remove vehicles back to the yard. We were ready to go, I would take the car and Les and Kevin had secured the farm machinery onto the trailer and had checked the damage to the truck's front bumper, was twisted but the truck was still in a road worthy condition.

The police agreed that the tractors could go back to the Ian's farm, Les drove the Artic unit to Ian's farm to remove the tractors and then drive the truck back to our yard to enable a Forensic check.

Then thinking about the damaging any finger prints in the truck cabin, we did a suspended tow to the farm dropped off the machinery then back. The brothers arrived back three hours later parking up the trucks and started the paperwork filling forms out.

Suzy turned in for work seeing us with our heads down in paperwork, made tea and serving to all in attendance. It was a welcome brew.

I went to my flat to clean up, while drying myself I was looking from the flat window over the yard.

Outside the yard on the road, a large silver car was parked in such a way that it could observe the yard and anyone working in the yard. I had a pair of binoculars in the flat somewhere finding them I took a squint at the occupants, and low and behold the two unsavoury characters thinking of the walrus and the carpenter character's I thought, Twiddle Dum and Twiddle Dee where appropriate names for them. Taking note of the registration plate, I called the police and explained what I had seen, and how they were watching us.

Just Three Lads

Then the car started to move, it drove down the street and into the yard gate the two characters getting out and walking into the office. I said to the officer on the telephone they have entered the yard. I must go.
my immediate thought was the protection of Suzy, she may be on her own, dressing quickly and getting to the office door in double quick time entering.
"Good morning how may I help you" I enquired,
"Yes" the smaller of the two spoke, reasonable eloquent for his appearance, I see that you do towing, would you by chance be able to move some machinery for us to "Ireland".
"Well, that was true but it was a service we offered when my father ran the business, we also had the wagons to do it, but I must say no, we now specialised in towing and accident recovery and secure vehicles storage".

The chap held his hand to his chin pondering what to say, "What about that truck in the yard that would move anything we had",

"Yes, it would however it is not ours and it was involved in an accident last night, and it is under Police control, so I could not help you with that even if I could".

"There is plenty of haulage companies around that would love the work I am assured of that. I looked at the wall where I kept business cards of companies offering services selected one and passed it to, Mr? Borrow was his reply
May I have your card, I have a couple of guys in mind they could do what you require, I am seeing them at a

haulier's dinner tomorrow night and could pass your card on".

"That is most decent of you" he concluded and gave me a business card with basic details, Mr Nickolas Borrow equipment movers and a mobile telephone and the address of 1a Lettersby Avenue Dublin. "Ok Mr Borrow I will ask a few firms I know and pass on your card and hopefully they will contact you".

Mr Nick Asked, do you sell vehicles from here. "Not really all the vehicles belong to somebody either the owners or insurance company, we get the storage charges.

As the stuff is here then gone the next day. We are looking for a small caravan type vehicle"?

"We have nothing like that for sale in fact I don't think we ever had",

Just then Farmer Ian walked in the door his bulky frame filled the office door aperture.

"Well, Well, Well, the last time I saw you two, you, were doing the same to me as you're doing to these guys, has he passed you a business card with his name of Nick Borrow from Lettersby avenue", the next thing, I lose machinery and it turns up on that truck you towed in you, these guys stole my tractors".

Mr Nick said "I am not staying here and getting spoke to like that".

"That's right you can go to the police station and get spoken to with menaces". Mr Nick tried to get past Ian, "not a chance". Twiddle Dum tried to get past by using his size, he rebounded off Ian's bulk and hit his head on the wall, and slithered down to the floor.

Just Three Lads

"What a wimp" Ian cried, Mr Nick takes a run at Ian, probably reckoning that an immovable object will move if it is hit in the correct place. Ian changed that rule and just by lifted his outstretched and clenched fist, the crack that I heard made me wince as the two immovable objects met, Mr Nicks chin and nose stopped abruptly on Ian's fist. Alas his torso legs and feet kept moving up to the level of Ian's arm, Mr Nicks body now achieving a horizontal position, but then the mass succumbed to the law of gravity and fell heavily to the floor.

A groan of disbelief slipped from his lips as he went into the land of dreams.

"Ian I am well impressed".

"It was a trick I learned working with animals, the occasional horse, or cow may run at you, so show who is in charge, when they see the fist, they always veer away at the last moment and then usually stop messing around".

"These two didn't learn that lesson".

Suzy sniggering spoke "They have now."

"Oh, sorry, dear; I did not see you there, you wouldn't have a pot of tea going would you, I need to take some pills"?

"Two minutes", Suzy said and off she went to produce the refreshments,

"Now Boss can you keep an eye on these two while I get something from the car", "Yes pleased to help", Ian was pretty quick on his pins for a chap so large ran out of the yard and came back in seconds, "I knew these would come in handy", Ian had in his mighty fist, a bunch of the largest tie wraps I have seen, he quickly bound

Just Three Lads

Twiddle Dum and Dee, as if he was restricting a pair thugs laid out on the floor in the office.

"Well now you got them what are you going to do"? Ian pulled out his mobile phone and pressed the digits for the police, explaining that he had caught the guys that stole his tractors, and his location. are they aggressive the police replied, not now we have them hog tied together, oh replied the officer, they would despatch a car immediately?

Twiddle Dum was the first to wake, looking around trying to break the restraints and get up he kept falling over, he started to shout and make a noise.

"That is not the way to act in front of a lady"; Ian pushed his hand in his pocket found a small roll of heavy duct tape and taped the offenders mouth shut. Suzy trying to keep a straight face served Ian with a cup of tea,

"Oh, I forgot to say there was somebody in the car parked in the gate, I pulled my car across the bows he won't get out and put a tie wrap through the door handles.

Would you by chance a have a slice of cake", Ian replied. Oh, Suzy replied "We only have rich tea biscuits".

DS Harper appeared "Good afternoon, whatsallthisthen, and did I hear tea and biscuits"?

"Well, I heard the police radio call to attend your place, and the mention of two thugs hog tied just had to be seen". Just then two more officers in blue came through the door. Suzy looking at the expanding group, then looked at me and whispered "We don't have that many cups if they all want tea"?

Just Three Lads

Ian quite confidently of his position and apprehending the criminal that stole his property, mentioned that there is a third one in the car and you will need these to get him out, passing them a pair of side cutters, they went out and brought back a female kicking and screaming blue murder. When both ladies eye met both exclaimed each other's name, Suzy getting the first word in, laid into her sister telling her what she thought about her...

Suzy was in full flow, coming out with some very close to the bone home truths. just knowing the Police would ask questions, I checked the CCTV Cameras for the recording, so rewinding I sat back to observe the action as it played out. Now it would appear that the truck we towed in belongs to Twiddle Dee, and he was sleeping soundly on the floor, so he gets the invoice for the call out last night, quickly totted up to £1,080.00 plus Vat, the grand total of £1296.00. I quickly wrote out an invoice, then I placed in on my desk for payment.

Suzy and Lizzy still going at it seemingly without stopping for breath, at times both coming to a pause, Suzy was the quicker to react and thinking on her feet, in fact she was turning out to be quite a woman, not a woman that will take any hassle. She also got the chance and gave Lizzy a swift kick in the shin bone then managed another as she turned her backside to her, cat fights are not nice   bit this one had a satisfying outcome. The two officers in blue decided that they should remove the three to the Police station and further enquiries can take place, the last to come to his senses was Mr Nick, I helped him up, I think he was playing possum and was keeping his eyes closed and taking notes on all matters that were discussed. Now that you are awake is the vehicle that we towed in last night yours? Snarling his reply at me "What of it".

"Well, it appears that you owe us some money for towing and how would you like to pay"? "How much is it"? "£1300.00 that cover's the recovery and storage till the end of the week, give or take extra days storage, I can take a credit card." "Give it to Sangster or give it to that posh tart Lizzy she is Sangster's Bitch".

Wow unexpectedly, a direct connection between the workers, the lover, and the boss, still as you are his representative you can settle the bill and we will give you a receipt, grudgingly he pulled his wallet from an inside pocket and pulled out a bunch of notes counted out the £1300, I stamped the receipt and passed it to him. "Do you want us to park the vehicle up for you at your place"? "Can you give this guy a call and he will come and get it for us". Mr Nick requested he passed me a card from his wallet,

Oh wow. the three wells again, it was a card of the garage round the corner from Sangster's office,

John Wade's Garage that old mate of mine, the one that came a calling and tried to steal something from the Motorhome, I considered my now ex mate.

Now a connection to a group of auto-mobile and farm equipment thieves.

He being such an upright honest garage owner, but also well known in the trade for his handling of dodgy specialised jobs of cutting and shutting vehicle bodies together.

In all the excitement I had totally forgotten to ask Ian what it was he had come for? He had only come in to make our acquaintance, and say thank you for the return of his tractors, his father, and daughter were on cutting the wheat as we spoke and he asked would there be a charge for delivering the tractors back to his farm? Ian your services helping this morning was good, I fact his tutorial and demonstration of the horse and cow treatment far outweighed any charges, in fact we were in his debt. this ok then I will be off and would it be ok to pop in occasionally when he was passing? "Yes, that would be ok" I would like to see him again.

As Ian departed, I saw a resemblance in him and the chap I saw in Sangster's office, then I remembered where I had seen tweedled Dum and Dee from, it was the Steroid twins.

Chapter 17

The commotion was moved to the police station, the police away drove the silver car the three occupants now hand cuffed, taken away in a police van. DS Harper, well that was entertaining, while the commotion was going on I took it upon myself to check out the vehicle I.D. and VIN numbers, and low and behold the silver car was not what it said on the vehicle register.

I mentioned to Harper that I have copy of the whole event if you wish to see it. "Ok best keep it safe we don't know which way this is going to go". I called on his phone written on the back the card that Mr nick gave me from John Wade and told him about the wagon that is here, and is to be returned to him. "I want nothing to do with it, "That wagon belongs to Sangster, get him to deal with it". and put the telephone down on me.

Oh, dear he must still be sore at me. I called Mr Sangster, he wasn't available to take my call, but he would be informed of the situation.

Suzy appeared with a couple of mugs of tea, and a box full of sandwiches, it's a bit late for dinner but these will do till later.

Over lunch she told me a lot more about her husband, and the driving work, that it now appears, he had, been quite naughty, and had no intention of telling her, Lizzy had boastingly implied that she had slept with him.

Suzy had taken it that she had meant Jim, her deceased husband.

But she also stated it didn't bother her; the modern lifestyle did seem to allow such liaisons. The telephone rang, Suzy taking the call, it was from the police control room, a full call out, three trucks required in three separate locations, calling the bros into the office, one job is a simple recover back to the yard job, I would take the flatbed truck, Les and Kevin can decide who did what with the heavy trucks. Telling Suzy, we normally close the place when we go out like this, I reckon she came to be with me, we closed the garage as normal. Then took off to the incidents, Suzy quite excited that she would see what we normally did every day, I did imply sometimes it is a straightforward pickup and go, then it can be an absolute nightmare. Arriving at the scene it was at a traffic light incident

A police car was at the scene, there was a small woman sat in the rear of the car, looking very sad. The officer told me the father was driving the car, they stopped for the traffic lights pulled the hand brake on then he died; the daughter, not realising what had happened, said, you are missing the lights get moving, but he wasn't going anywhere. The ambulance has just taken him to the hospital. she didn't want to go.

I the enquired where does she want the car delivered too, she said that she is not sure, as her father was the only one that drove, and she the daughter was a timid type of person and was too frightened to learn, could we take the car and sell it for us. she handed me a business card I gave her my card and I said I would be in touch.

The Officer said he would take the lady home and see that she was ok, he also gave me a note with the lady's address and telephone number, so we could contact he later, Suzy said she could drive the car back, for me to save loading, I said that would be nice but she wasn't insured, and the call out had been placed, ten minutes later we were on our way back to the yard. Suzy looking at the car through the back window, that is a nice car what would she take for it, in her state a bag of jelly babies, but I can check the price when I get back it won't be a lot of money. Suzy asked "if I would like to come for dinner tonight, she said the girls were having a sleepover at their pals and the sleep over may last most of the coming weekend, oh that would be nice, she said I heard you say you were going to a hauliers dinner Saturday evening, I was going to ask you to come then, but I can see you in your suit drinking and having a good time with your pals".

"I did say it was a dinner but there is a dance afterwards as well, would you like to come with me tomorrow"?

Suzy thought that was a brilliant idea, and she hadn't been dancing for years. She leant over and kissed me on my ear, with an mwah type of kiss the sound still ringing in my ears as I pulled into the yard.

Kevin was back with a bus on the back of the truck, the front part of the roof torn back and serious damage to the rest of the bus. "Was the old low bridge on the back road short cut"?

"Yes, also full of pensioners on a trip to the coast, lots of walking wounded the bus is still full of personal effects".

"Best cover the bus", the Press will be looking for ghoulish pictures.

Les arrived back with one wagon on tow a fully loaded 40 feet with trailer with large coils of steel wire flapping loosely on the back, the support legs on the trailer were damaged, making it difficult to unload from the tractor unit. He called Nobby to get the fork lift truck and support the trailer with wooden blocks so they could unhitch and then repair the tractor unit, Nobby sprang into action loading blocks of wood from the corner of the yard knobby was one of those guys you show him once and he knows how to tackle a problem.

Then he uncoupled the articulated tractor unit, and drove it into the garage and started to prepare the damage for a repair.

Kevin appeared half an hour later, reversing the container wagon into the yard, a huge tear in the steel side curtain.

He manoeuvred it round and parked it by the side of the trailer with the loose coils. The yard was getting full; four long vehicles take up some space, and the cars from Previous accidents had not been cleared, next week, I will try to clear the rubbish out, but still a full yard, pay's storage fees.

Suzy leaving for home blew me a kiss, "See you around 7"?

"Will do, do you want a bottle of wine for the meal brought in"?

"Yes, I love red", with a wink she was gone.

Les asked what was to happen with the articulated belonging Mr Sangster, well that so called mate of mine, John Wade had told us he wanted nothing to do with it, and it should go back to Mr Sangster's office or his house. I don't really care. Or we wait and see what he does either way we get paid. I don't like the man although I have never met him, but I have met his thugs.

Farmer Ian sorted them out, I have never seen anything so funny, telling Les details of the event, he was laughing, I would have liked to have seen that happen.

Just Three Lads

Suddenly a scream of tyres, Kevin's new car rocketed out of the garage making a beeline for the gate, just before the gate the car was swung round, the driver using the hand brake to ensure a tight turn, had totally miss calculated the turn, and slid backwards into a pile of old tyres, which made then topple onto the car. now old tyres collect all sorts of rubbish, water, and crap, spilling out onto the car. Les and I running to the driver's aid, Kevin gingerly climbing out of the car, looked at the mess.

"Oh Bugger, I wished I had not done that. But it does go well"; the three of us started to re stack the tyres this time not going so high up the wall. Kevin moved his car to near the jet wash punched the start button and started to clean off the mess on his car, within a minute he had his new beast gleaming again. Quickly reversing it back into the garage, he put it away for the night.

Les announced he has a hot date, and did not want to be disturbed

Kevin was watching a movie and was on call for the evening.

I was going out to dinner. Standing in the shower letting the warm water wash away the muck of the day, I like to shave at the same time it is refreshing, always makes me feel better afterwards; towelling myself dry the reflection in the mirror revealed that the bruising around the eye and eyebrow was hardly noticeable, but a new bruise was showing on my shoulder and ribs, two marks were starting to show on my chests like oval round marks, where had they came from, my memory evaded me. Selecting some dark blue slacks and a tailored dark blue shirt, a pair of light tan moccasin shoes, I felt ready to go and eat.

Just Three Lads

The choice of vehicle was down to the small wrecker truck, company pickup or van, taking the van I whistled my way round to Suzy, stopping at the off-licence shop, I procured a fine bottle of Red, some posh looking chocolates, plus a bag of liquorice chunks, and then continued my way.

Suzy letting me in to a gorgeous smell of food being prepared, as she closed the door, I heard a secondary click Suzy had locked the door. "Will I be safe with the door locked? you will be safe from any outside females was her reply, I rubbed my hands together. Thinking a spot of hand cream would be nice, but some like the strong hand touch.

An aroma wafted past my nose but could not place it, Suzy dressed in her apron with bare legs and high heels, from the front that is all it looked she was wearing, this was going to be an interesting meal, she showed me in to the lounge and then taking the wine from me placed it on the table, picking up another tray she reversed into the kitchen,

"How do you like your steak"? "Medium rare please",

"Do you like onions with the steak"?

"Yes please, shall I uncork the wine"?

"If you want" but she giggled

"Why are you giggling"?

"It is a screw top"...

"OK shall I pour the wine"? "Yes please" the table was laid for two in the corner of the room, The glasses were on a small tray. Pouring two glasses of wine, I tasted one, it was nice; I do hope that Suzy liked it as well.

Just Three Lads

She entered carrying two wooden plates of sizzling steaks laid on cast iron platters, carefully placing them on the table, ok please sit down offering me a seat, she walked over to the window and pulled the curtains them pressed a button on her little music centre. coming over to the table she took of her pinny, to reveal, a very nice mini skirt and a skimpy blouse top, leaving nothing to the imagination.

"You look absolutely stunning".

"Thank you, kind Sir, please sit down"

Quickly we tucked into our meal the steak was perfect, just the correct number of onions, the cheapo screw top red wine was agreeable with the steak. The meal and company were perfect, I even became so bold to say so. A slight blush came over her face, it made her look very attractive, her nipples were becoming obvious through her blouse.

Her wine needed topping up, picking up the bottle I indicated would she like some more, she took a deep breath and sighed "Yes please". Pouring the wine she remarked on the wine, where did I get it from the off-licence, it was suggested by the shop keeper as one of the best ones. Suzy just nodded agreement as she was finishing her steak took another drink, savouring the wine she remarked excellent. Finishing her meal, I also was finishing off as well, I collected the plates and took them into the kitchen placing them into the sink, I washed my hands and as I dried them, Suzy caught my eye and said in a low voice

"Now I have an option for afters, ice cream, or me." what flavour is the ice cream? "Vanilla with raspberry sauce". "Shall we enjoy both", I replied. "Oh, I am glad"

Just Three Lads

Slipping past me in the doorway I gave her a kiss she responded immediately thrusting her breasts into my chest, her tongue slipped between my lips and our embrace lasted longer than I had intended, but I enjoyed the feeling. Sitting at the table, I was presented with a plate two scoops of ice cream with two spots of raspberry sauce. That looks delightful very tempting, she was just bout collapsing with her giggles, "ok come on let me know what the giggles are about", her blush increased, as did her nipple size. Thinking is this the result of the red wine, or something else, I held out my hand and offered her to the sofa where we sat and looked at each other, her eyes were sparkling and she was biting her lip. She leant forward and kissed me on the brow, and then I noticed the bruise on her face was well disguised with makeup. "I see your bruise is getting better", "Yes" she replied as she was unbuttoning my shirt, spreading my shirt open, she gave my chest kisses and a kiss to one of my nipples, it stung and made me jump. "What is the matter" and she sat up to see what she had touched with her lips, noticing the two oval red marks her finger ran across the red marks on my chest, where did they come from? "I have no idea" She kissed me tenderly on the marks, there they are better, I wonder if they were from the machine the paramedics used, "From the what"?

I asked, I was feeling concerned and apprehensive "Well you know the day you collapsed on the bedroom wall knocking yourself out"? "Yes, yes what happened"?

"Well, the Paramedics had to use that defibrillator machine to resuscitate you".

"Oh, wow is that what the pain was"? "You remember"?

"Yes, I was watching it and felt pain stab in my chest".
"What you mean you watched it"? "I had a dream in which I was stood by the side of you all watching people work on somebody lay out on the floor".
Her hand went across her mouth," you have had one"?
"A one what"
"An out of body experience".
"I don't remember"
"Well, you have, what else do you remember"?
"Do you have another sister"?
"Yes, Clarissa but she is the sister in-law and you already met both.
" Suzy cuddled in turning on her back letting my hand fall over her breast, she moved her top slightly then moved my hand onto her breast. I thought of what I could remember,
"There was the lady from the motorhome dream", "The one that kissed you from the gloom"?
"Yes, and she did it again, then there was a dark-haired man sitting cross legged sitting in a huge area like a waiting room in a railway station, but the room was vertical, other people were moving up, and some going down, and some just motionless, but he was the only one sitting cross legged."
Making the tip of my finger circle her breast her nipple grew harder and a slight moan came from her mouth, she responded to the touch making the other breast available to the hand. "What else happened in the dream"?
"There were more stabs of pain and everything was going slow, it seemed like I was there waiting as well, I looked and I too was sitting cross legged. Looking at the man he saw me looking at him and spoke, his lips moved

but no voice came forth he spoke again and still no voice, he kept pointing to his wedding ring finger and repeating the same words, I managed to work out what he said."

"By now Suzy turned around and was sitting astride me on the sofa",

He said, "Tell her I know where it is"

"No, no that wasn't it, I went over the image in my brain with my eyes closed, mouthing the words again.

"I am sorry for not coming back, and he said James T knows where it is".

"Oh my god" Suzy cried.

"There was another thing I remember"?

"What is that my darling"?

"The lady in the dream and camper",

"Yes dearest", "She, looked a bit like you and I am sure she had two earrings in one ear, one in the other, a slight crooked nose and the tip of her index finger was missing". Oh No! Suzy gasped, "Mum", I felt her body go limp and she fell onto me, her head cracking my head as she landed. "Ouch, not again, the bruise area started throbbing, her eyes were closed and she was breathing faintly, I could feel her heart beating through my chest, she was deathly pale and motionless.

I managed to move her enough to one side, enabling me slip out from underneath her. I returned with a glass of water.

She was still out cold; the room was now chilling. I lifted her from the sofa and carried her upstairs, I worked out which was her bedroom, I laid her on to the bed, throwing the duvet over her. the water had survived me carrying her upstairs, that I placed on her bedside table.

Just Three Lads

I could feel something on my brow; looking in the bathroom mirror, I got a shock, where we had cracked our heads, a cut had appeared, in my case was bleeding. Dabbing the wound with a damp pad of toilet paper it stopped almost instantly, I walked back to the bedroom and saw there was some blood on her brow, I wiped the blood away, this also causing her to stir slightly she murmured something and turned herself over on to her tummy, her clothes revealed the lower part of her back and cheeks her backside, I could see enough to know that the difference between her and her sister is the birthmark or mole that I observed the previous day.

I waited a while and then made a cold compress from a hand towel, held this on her neck and head she came round from her faint.

Her eyes opened quickly looking around recollecting where she was.

"You fainted downstairs, and became cold, you were shivering so I brought you here. "What happened to your head, as she noticing my cut, you struck your brow with mine, I came off worse". "

Oh, I am sorry, I don't remember what happened".

You were describing what happened to me when I was unconscious in my flat; you then said "Oh my god and collapsed on me".

"Oh dear, you must have terrible thoughts of me, but I am not feeling that well, do you mind, if you go home, I feel terrible.

Of course, I don't mind, kissing her on soft lips, she was asleep before I got to the bedroom door.

I checked the back door, was locked, locking the front door behind me, I put the door key through the letter box, then drove slowly home.

My brain, was racing the options what might have been, I am sure she wanted me, as I her.

Then the dream I had relived, the shock that I remembered. The last word Suzy said before she collapsed "Mum".

I felt safe and secure in my flat, I was falling asleep with various thoughts pounding round in my brain.

Chapter 18

It was the end of the week; and today was Saturday, usually a busy day, it was remarkable that there were no calls for the Friday evening, there must have been a good evening on the TV to keep everybody at home. My thoughts were confused about Friday's fiasco, how Suzy had managed to cope I didn't know, impulsively calling her mobile it rang until the answer phone switched in, then she spoke saying, whoever was calling please leave a message.

In all this anxiety and stress, this lady was under my skin, just hearing her voice would settle my impulses, surmising that she was probably still asleep.

Thinking of what vehicle to use tonight to go to the dinner, I thought if I wish to have a couple of drinks driving was out and Suzy probably would not want to go in the works van, it was now my personal transport, and unless we went in the Motorhome, it was going to be a taxi or Suzy's car. I even thought about swiping Kevin's car, but he would fret if I did. The morning passed quickly, even making comment to Les that the breakdowns were quiet, "Don't knock it, I don't mind the rest." An old couple came into the yard and requested could they go into the crashed bus to get their personal belongings, I asked them to come back next week, as the tour operator, was coming to clean all personal property, and deliver it back to the passengers, the lady looked at the bus and said, "we were sitting just there, pointing at the only window left in one side, I think I was lucky as everyone else got covered in glass from the broken windows. She continued to tell us how they were looking forward to the trip the age of herself, her husband, Doris down the street and her 5 cats, and what she had for her tea last night, and wound it up with saying she had broken her false teeth, then before I could stop her, she slipped them from her mouth and displayed the crack in the teeth plate. I ushered her out quickly, there are something's I don't wish to see and false teeth in two parts or one part is quite high on the list.

She returned claiming could her husband have his holiday case, as all his underpants were in there and he needed a clean pair... Les saw my dilemma, and asked the woman her name and what seat did she have?

The old lady gave Les the ticket, inspecting it he immediately saw a problem, then looked at the lady, this ticket is not for that coach trip, this is for a trip two months ago, get out of this office, you wicked people, and then proceeded to escort them out of the office and off the premises; shouting after them that he was keeping this ticket and passing it onto the police. times are bad, when you can't trust little old ladies, and they turn out to be thieves, trying to claim other people's luggage from a crash site. Suzy then appeared, "What have those two been up to?" nodding her head in the direction of the old couple still arguing with themselves as they walked away from the yard. Les quickly explained the confidence trick they had just tried on us.

Suzy laughed, why it is accidents bring out the nastiness in people. "Well, how are you? did you sleep well"? "I slept well, I don't remember much one part seemed like a horror dream, and I needed something for this evening dinner, and just had to go to town to get something nice.

Just Three Lads

"Would you like to see what I have got"? Thinking I have already seen, and it is all nice, "I found it in the posh shop in the town, absolute bargain, it only needs a stitch", "What you were wearing or not wearing last night was pretty cool",
"That was specially just for you, that would be far to revealing for tonight".
"Oh, err what needs a stitch"?
"Oh, the new dress, well it is new to me, a lady trying it on, her heel caught the hem and the stupid woman had ripped the back of the dress, but with some delicate stitching; I will repair that easily when I get home.
"I will come for you at six thirty, we have half an hour drive to get there; shall we go in the Motorhome or the works van"? Suzy looked back at me, Motorhome, and then we can use it to sleep in, if we drink too much and drive back in the morning. Cool advanced thinking, should we put some bedding in the Motorhome for the sleep over. "Give me the keys, Suzy holding her hand out to receive them, she went to inspect the Motorhome coming back with a list. "We need all on that list for in there, or we stay in a hotel, and Don't even consider picking me up in the works van".
Oh, so the tow truck is out of the question then? Suzy turned on her heels and walked out to her car. I must admit as I watched her leave, she has a lovely movement with the swing of her hips. Les whispering, you're getting caught, completely. Realising what he said, I grinned, possibly but she is exciting, and I am enjoying the ride, and the breath of fresh air. Looking at the list of what she wanted, I walked to the corner shop and filled the list. The Duvets I got from the corner supermarket....

Just Three Lads

With the list filled, I decided to take the rest of the afternoon off, and get a few things for myself, from Donald's, Gentleman outfitters, Donald may have been a raving homosexual, but really knew his business, when fitting a new set of threads to the male body. he knew just how to smooth down the suit to fit the male figure. He kitted me out with the best kit he had, taking a small mortgage from my credit card. I drove back, looked in on the yard, stowed my new threads in the flat, taking a shower, and deciding on that special shower gel, that you keep for best, then you find it ran out months ago.

thinking back to that evening, brought a smirk on my face, I didn't know, a woman could get in such a position.

back to reality, soap it is. I always said that A good shower, is as good as sex. I think that a sleep, before the evening would be a good idea, I slipped into my bed, and quickly dozed off, slight noises kept waking me but I dozed a shallow sleep, and woke around five feeling fully refreshed. I dressed and felt a million dollars.

I felt hungry, but I decided to forego a sandwich before I left, the food served at these dinners was always brilliant, best, not to spoil my appetite. The shopping, that Suzy wanted was already in the Motorhome, I called at the corner shop, and purchased a packet of Chocolate Hobnob biscuits; placing them in the driver's side door pocket, then continued towards Suzy's house.

Quickly knocking on the door, I heard her calling me to enter, adding she will be down in two minutes.

I kept standing to keep the crease in my new threads.

Just Three Lads

A small voice asked from behind, will I do. turning to see a vision of loveliness, Suzy adorned in her new attire, displayed the strapless evening gown cut just on the knee, with a small clutch bag in matching colour, with high stiletto heeled shoes, observing the vision, I was going to say a cheeky remark, I was dumbfounded, she looked a million dollars, I am not sure what the feeling is called that I was experiencing but it had stirred within my loins.

Suzy viewed her date for the evening making me twirl around, then did some adjusting to my suit and flicking the odd hair off my shoulder and straightened my tie. I am impressed, you do scrub up well, if you play your cards right tonight you may just win that prize. Pouting her lips, she blew me a kiss trying to wink and finish off the statement.

She ended up blinking at me.

A blink, wow, I have had the odd wink thrown at me, but never a suggestive blink before.

We both laughed and we locked her house and headed off to the venue both in good spirits.

Chapter 19

Escorting the lady to her carriage for the evening, we drove toward the next town where the posh bunfight was taking place.

During the drive Suzy was unusually quiet, remarking on some landmark as we passed them, strangely quiet,

"Are you ok"?

"Yes, it is a long time since I dressed up for an evening out", It was lovely to make the effort and get ready, also it is nice to be going with a man that has noticeably also made the effort.

Stopping at the traffic lights, "I turned, my head looked at her, do you realise that I think that you are lovely, and I was so happy when you accepted to come with me tonight, and you look stunning.

I was enjoying the view of Suzy in her dress, sat in the Front part of the RV, I missed the traffic lights as they changed. Yet the vehicle behind, reminded me, by blowing his horn, and gesticulating he was ordering two pints.

Suzy moved closer to me and kissed me on the lips, and mentioned "You are so kind thank you".

Then sat back down in her seat. The shock of that statement and the scene in the dream sent a warning bell in my brain.

I was now on edge; I became very aware of driving only relaxing when I drove into the car park of the hotel and dance hall. Parking the Motorhome away from the hall, in a quiet part of the car park, but still under a flood light, we disembarked and secured out transport for the evening, then made for the hotel entrance. as we started up the steps, a squeal of tyres as a large black car swung into the park taking the first available space, which was also a disabled parking spot, the doors flew open, two men dressed to the nines, escorted two ladies, also dressed in fine fettle, or just to say dressed, were already in party mode. The men walking quickly, towards the hotel entrance, the distinct sound of the stiletto heels tripping along behind them, changed as they went from stone tiles to carpet, this four, gave the impression of people in a hurry. We let them pass us by, giggles and shrieks of merriment as one of the ladies put her hand out and nipped her date's bottom, they entered the ballroom.

Suzy spotted this action and decided it was a customary requirement gave my bottom a little nip as well.

"Thank you, madam that is just, what I needed, I am glad I wasn't facing the other way".

"I thought it was the custom those two both did it". I whispered we are entering the Ballroom not the bottom room. Suzy let out a single cry of joy, and sniggered as we walked in.

We entered the hotel and met a large gathering of people, a few cries of greetings and introductions abound for the next twenty minute, waiters walking round with drinks for everyone. Suzy chose an orange juice, instead of wine, I also followed her example. It was good to see old friends and chat, business problems, seem to be the main topic, sharing with the closest of business friends, insight to the latest cons and tricks that some of the light-fingered people were up to.

Just Three Lads

Suzy was introducing herself to colleague's wives if I hadn't; she was getting on famously. The dinner gong boomed out its invitation, is always a ceremony checking where we were sitting, and seeing who our table companions were.

We were near the top table, with the outgoing president and new president elect of the haulier's association, speeches by those drones were a drawn-out affair. If you were quick enough you could make the bar and stay there before the president stood up, as he would drivel on for the forty minutes.

Suzy pointed at the head table, look who is sitting on that table Mr Sangster, in brackets President Elect.

How the bollocks did that crook get into that position.

I observed we were sitting with a couple of out spoken chums on our table, I was happy with that. Suzy already had chosen her seat, where she was partially hidden from the gaze of Mr Sangster. Sitting between her and Sangster, I took out my telephone and sent a text message to DS Harper, informing him of Sangster's new position in the Road Haulage Association.

A few minutes later he sent a text back, saying he would meet me in the Bar in an hour or so, give the dinner chance to settle and be cleared away. He would be very interested in what he had to say, and he would like me to put some questions to him. Could this be an entrapment technique?

I thought, now would an officer of the law, try to catch a crook in such a way.

The excellent meal was ending I managed to get through it with no soup dribble on my tie, it was noticeable that the ex-president was shuffling papers and getting ready to stand and deliver his retirement speech. one of our table guests decided that the bar was a better place to be.

I saw Harper hovering in the doorway, saying to Suzy "I will be back going for a personal break". Suzy also required similar relief, trying to do this in a quiet mode back fire, when one of our larger than life and pure loud gob table companion had to say loudly, He was going to take a piss, did anyone wish to join him, and said to his friend Bob, it's your round get them in while I am away.

The spotlights turned to my table with such a crude statement. Some people laughed and some just looked, but I noticed all on the top table were looking in our direction.

I met DS Harper on the way back from the loo, even he remarked you can do without announcements like your table companion voiced.

We chattered over what was going to be said,

Why don't you come and sit on the table, there is a vacant seat next to me and I have a couple of chums that will be able to put the point across for you, as well as I can."

He agreed whole heartily with the offer, taking his seat he was just in time for Coffee and the customary after eight chocolate delight.

The outgoing President finishing off with his customary joke, it happened that it was the same joke he cracked when he became the president a year previous.

He described the new incoming President as bright new leading light in the Haulage Association, and the future way forward, both in his thinking and ideas for the future.

Just Three Lads

Mr Sangster stood up; a couple of jeers from another table, Harper looked at me, "There, is a turn-up for the books we are not alone." Mr Sangster seemed to love the limelight; I was sure he increased in size as he started to deliver his speech. Suzy had persisted but was getting bored, started rubbing her foot up and down my leg under the table, a little distracting but enjoyable. She shuffled her chair closer to me, and let her hand rest on my thigh, and proceeded to make small movement with her hand.

Keeping my hand under the table cloth, I also rubbed her thigh, not realising her intention she had pulled the material higher up her leg.

The tease had opened her legs slightly and pressed my hand between them, all the while her face was unemotional.

She was set to play, and there was no way I could stop her without attracting attention to us.

Then she noticed DS Harper, and whispered do you see who is sitting next to you, yes, I replied, I invited him to sit with us, by the way nice Beaver, well I thought Suzy was going to have a sneezing fit, she tried to stifle the snort, but fortunately made a grab for my top pocket handkerchief, she was lucky it was a real hanky and not a trimmed bit stapled to a carboard strip.

Suzy turned her attention to my ear, and quietly blowing into it, I thought it a fly buzzing around and I was just about to waft it away, when she to play another game. And was just about to start when, President elect, Sangster raised his voice, waffled on about safety, security, and the theft of loads.

Just Three Lads

Then launched into a scheme how high value loads could be registered and carry the all-new tracking devices, with them linked to a central or regional control centre.

He had office space available and one centre be located there.

That brought comments of Rubbish and Don't be silly, Sangster noticing this decided to pick on one of the objectors, a small one wagon band, a self-haulier, his beef was that small hauliers, had enough regulations, without being told as and when then what routes they had to take.

Sangster had a go at him delivering a damming cursor towards him. "There was no need for that" I whispered. One chap from our table asked how did they intend policing the loads and what if any charges would this service attract.

A waffle of sorts came back with a suggested sliding scale, Then DS Harper voiced "If such an operator of such impeccable security would have to have a squeaky-clean history in the business.

Would the Mr Sangster be able to demonstrate his own history to ensure members had trust with him?

The statement landed, backed up with a few little cheers, and cat calls and then the good old-timer Hear, Hear.

Sangster quickly trying to save his sinking ship, followed the statement, more waffle and he would personally guarantee that his history was clean and secure.

Then mentioned, he was an officer of the high court with him being a Solicitor.

Just Three Lads

One chap from across the ballroom called out what grade of Solicitor is that then?
Great guffaws of laugh abounded with the final statement. Nearly every operator had felt the charges, Solicitors charge for their alleged Legal services.
Mr Sangster won the vote, unbelievable was sworn in as the next year President, despite numerous objections, I wonder how many votes he had bought,
I on the other hand managed to remain quiet and observe without being noticed. As well as enjoy in having my tummy button caressed, by a marauding finger.

The meeting was over, the ballroom was re arranged and prepared, the resident Quartet struck up with music to entice you and partner onto the dance floor.
Sitting out the first dance I listened to Harper and a few others talk about the subjects that had been brought up in the speech. Harper says, Sangster is up to something, I can't work out what his perspective. A lot of what they talked about had no connection with my business.

Suzy whispered in my ear, I want to dance, will you dance with me?
Standing, I held out my hand towards Suzy, May I have the honour of this dance, she graciously accepted, then she walked me onto the dance floor, it was a waltz, it had been a long time, since I had done any dancing.
But for this lady I would try, I could feel Suzy holding me close, she expertly guided me through a few moves, then said let's try and see how the next dances go.
Ready for the next dance, we would give it our best performance, to wow the rest of the dinner guests, only

to have, the band leader calls a 20-minute break. What can you do in such circumstances, I gave her a big twirl round and walked her back to the table. You looked as if you enjoyed that Harper remarked.

"I will have to go, thanks for the Heads up on this guy, he will have to be watched.

I did say we still have one of his trucks in our yard.

and he hasn't called us", Harper looking puzzled, "What truck.

"The one that that the two stolen tractors loaded on it, the bridge crash yesterday morning, the ones stolen from Farmer Ian.

"I know nothing about that, why don't we go and ask him if he asks about me, I work for you as a driver."

Suzy went to powder her nose, we went and addressed Sangster. It was difficult to get to him as he seems to have men guarding his back, finally I managed to get his attention, I referred to the telephone message, I was waiting for about the return of his truck.

He said "Who are you"? I explained that I was the recovery company that has recovered and is now storing his articulated flatbed vehicle.

"He was unaware of any calls, then claimed that truck had been stolen.

As I was holding it, he would like it back".

"I will contact the police tomorrow, but it was involved in a theft, an accident where the driver, absconded from the scene of the accident. Now you say it was reported stolen after the fact, I contacted you".

Sangster snarled back at me. "Are you trying to imply that I am involved in this occurrence?

Just Three Lads

DS Harper remarked "We are just trying to find out where you want the truck delivered".
"But as the boss is reporting to the police tomorrow, we will have to wait and see what they say"
about delivering the vehicle anywhere.
We wished him a pleasant evening, and withdrew from his company.
Did you notice Sangster had built up heels on his shoes and his hair was back combed to make him taller. I replied to Harper such a short arse, little man syndrome you reckon. As I walked Harper out to the foyer, he was confused, I am going to investigate this man, there is some dealings, that will connect if we cross ref information. I will catch up later when I have some info worth, talking about. Suzy requested a drink as she came to find me, and slid her hand in mine, pulled me close to her, blew a small jet of air in my ear. "What would you like"? "A Brandy it would go down nicely, after the meal, I want you totally to myself, for the rest of the evening", standing on tip toe she gave me a kiss in my ear, then as she pulled back, she pulled a tissue from her purse and wiped the lipstick mark from my cheek and ear lobe. Suzy pulled me onto the dance floor and we danced the rest of the dances, stopping for one and finishing our brandy's we returned to the floor and danced all the wrong dances to the wrong music but really enjoying the last waltz. The room was thinning of the guests and maybe it was time to slip away, all the friends I had on the table had already gone, we agreed to leave, as we were walking out, I noticed a wall sign stating car park this way, we took the side door as the main entrance was crowded with guests. Walking hand

in hand then hand in pocket Suzy's stroking what shouldn't be when you're pointing in the wrong direction, we finally made the privacy of the Motorhome. Once inside she said "you have treated me like a lady tonight, now it's time to stop", "My turn, to make you feel wanted by a lusty woman as she entertains her man". She went round the motorhome and made sure all the curtains were closed, the doors locked, and the roof vent was open. "We were at last on our own, the most desirable woman, was standing in front of me, with a very cheeky grin on her face, and her hands on her hips. I turned the passenger seat round facing into the Motorhome chamber, switched on the car radio, I had already inserted some easy listening CD's anticipating an evening like this, it was a warm evening, I was going to take off my Jacket. "Sorry Sir, one may not remove any clothing, before the star. Suzy moving to the music proceeded to a strip in front of me, I have never had a personal striptease before, and found this most stimulating, I can see why lap dancing clubs were popular, to have a personal lap dancer is spectacular. Suzy had a magnificent body, her breasts had a bounce to them that she managed to use to her benefit, and my enjoyment. Sitting astride my lap she tugged at my bow tie, "It won't undo it is a clip on, she found the catch and removed it, she held it in her hand saying real ones I can use as a whip what do I do with this bow, I replied she could put her foot here, which she did, I adjusted the neck strap fitted the bow tie around her upper thigh, slowly sliding it up her thigh, until it was held firmly.
She then returned, and slowly relieved of my Jacket, and placed it on a coat hanger, then returned to her task, the

shirt went the same way, and joined the jacket, also my trousers were the next to go the journey, leaving me in pants socks and shoes, the leg was lifted and the shoe and sock removed, she slid the sock though each toe slowly and then each toe was sucked slowly, then the treatment was repeated, to the other foot. Now the only thing between us, was the pants that we wore, the way Suzy intended they would be removed, in a very short time. Starting at my neck, I was plied with kisses, all round my neck and shoulders, she continued down my chest, stopping at my nipples taking care with the marks caused by the cardiac resuscitation machine. then sitting astride my lap, she made her breasts available for my mouth, her nipples were rock hard by now, as was I, this bulge did not go unnoticed, she moved her hips up and down my crotch, moving and pulling my pants, until I was free, with one quick movement of her hand, her pants were released, the object of both our desires were finally ready, and waiting to be make each other's acquaintance. She found the seat reclining lever, pressing it, then she pushed me backwards into a horizontal position, finally stood above me, and located me in her vagina, she slowly circled me with the hips, each fourth time she circled she moved down a little, taking her time, and constant pressure, she achieved full penetration, then continued with the hip movement, keeping herself quiet I could hear her stifling her screams of ecstasy, her hands fell upon my shoulders ,and her breasts swung across my chest, they were so soft yet firm, her hands had turned back on themselves, as she tried to prolong her climax. It was too late, I took hold of her hips and bottom, and pulled her towards me, her breath was short and gasping, as she perspired then gracefully collapsed upon me. We lay holding each other for a long time; I started to feel the cooling air of the night, in the bedroom, a warm bed was waiting for us. I took her in my arms then carried her the short way.

Snuggling in we made love again this time it was my turn to climax and pass enjoyment to each of us. later during the night, I was woken by a slight movement in the middle of the bed, her hips were moving, she was trying to excite me without me stirring, I didn't make it obvious I was awake, and I let her take her fantasy or erotic pleasure, finally moving her hips away, her mouth took its place.

I played her so gently; she achieved her climax. She releases a sigh and muttered he was tired yet managed four times.

The luminous clock digital figures glowed six thirty, I mulled over the evening's events, I was very impressed, in fact a lot more than very.

My mind was awake, looking at the watch again, still 6:30, then a twinge in my groin, made me aware that at 6:30, sex hurty as well, it was glorious pain, I had enjoyed the foreplay, and the love play.

Thinking how it would be to have love like that, all the time, would be an excellent idea. the clock still displayed 6:30. I was in the hour-long minute time. my mind racing and still 6:30 was displayed.

Then a quiet moan came from the back of the Motorhome, looking towards Suzy she was fast asleep with a smile on her lips, then the moan came again but not from her. looking from the rear window, I could see only two cars were left in the car park. One at the far end, and one in the middle, in the shadow cast by the street lamp, I could see a foot sticking out from the shadow, straining my eyes to make out more detail, the leg moved and a weak "Help Me" was heard, warm hands rested on my shoulder,

"What is it"? Someone in the car park, is laid out by the side of that car, quickly pulling on my trousers then finding a sweater from the cupboard, I grabbed a torch, unlocked the door, and proceeded to investigate the call for Help.

I left the van, then heard Suzy call out, be careful my darling.

Shining the torch, I could see the rest of the body, a man he was dressed in a dinner suit, as I got closer, I could see dried blood covering his face and chest, initially I thought the guy must have been inebriated, slipped, and banged his head then fallen by the side of his car.

"Hello mate I called out to him, did you fall"?

The figure lifted his head and looking in my direction said, "No some bastard clobbered me;" shining my torch around him nothing was laid around, I saw the mark on his face in the corner of the car, where presumably his head had hit as he went down.

"Do you think you can get up"?

"I will with help"

Helping him to his feet, I noticed the light come on in the Motorhome, come with me, and let's see what we can do for your face.

Sitting him down in the seat which had seen the previous night's action he was covered in blood.

Suzy already with some warm water and a towel bathed his face and tidied him up the best she could.

Just Three Lads

You have a lovely lump on the back of your head,
"Aye that is where, the bastard got me"
"Where did this happen"?
"In the car park by my car, not the one where you found me, my is in the front car park".
I am sure it was somebody, from the dance that hit me, but I could not be sure.
Now I recognised him, it was the quiet chap, that had asked the first annoying question from President Sangster. "Hello I am called Matt; sorry to be a nuisance, my Mrs. always said my gob, would get me in bother."

A hot tea was thrust into Matt's hand, that may put some warmth back into you, if you have laid in the car park all night.
Suzy retrieved the first aid kit, and selected a plaster for the cut on his forehead, sorry about your shirt I have nothing here to remove the blood.
"Aye, lass don't worry yourself, it will all come out in the wash."
"Well, I have taken up too much of your time, I must get going and get home, or my wife will think I have a woman".
I slipped one of my business cards, into Matt's top pocket, then helped him to his car.
he was getting better by the second,
"By, your lass makes a grand cup of tea, I could fight for England now".
"Are you sure you will be ok to drive home"?
"What was leaking has stopped, I feel much better" with that he opened his car clambered in started the engine and drove off up the road.

Just Three Lads

Chapter 20

Looking round the car park, there was nothing to see in the dim light, as I walked back, I felt something hard under my foot, looking down, it was part of a cuff link, picking it up I put it in my pocket, back in the motorhome, I slipped off my clothes, then eagerly slipped back into bed. Suzy cuddled up to me, asked how was he. I think he perked up very well after you had made him some tea, he recovered incredibly quickly, then after you bent down to get the first aid kit from the floor cupboard, you revealed more that was modest. Suzy whispered, oh dear", and slid her hand down my tummy to my groin, taking firm hold, she played and teased my member, until it was ready to go again. Then once more the greedy delights of a woman with intention took the lead. It will be nice when at a future date we can do this again, I will take the initiative. We managed to sleep until around 10 in the morning, the comfort of that Motorhome is very good, asking Suzy what she was doing for the rest of the day, ladies things cleaning washing, the worst bit the ironing then whatever the girls come back with, they will have to be tended too. We breakfasted in the Hotel, mentioning to the manager about the chap we had discovered in the car park and tending his wounds, he said he would make a note of it in the diary if anything was to come of it. As we walked back to the vehicle from the hotel, a glint of shiny steel from under the front tyre caught my eye, upon closer inspection a small but long screw was resting in front of the front tyre, also one resting on the ground behind the same tyre. Looking at the remaining tyres, there were screws sitting in the same locations. Scanning around the ground I was looking for anything else untoward that may give me a puncture. Suzy helped me collect them, she was intrigued how had I spotted them, "it was something I always did", I replied to her question, the ground was now clear of the little screws, Suzy had a good amount in her hands she put them in a small cup, taking a look at the tyres in case I had already got a screw stuck in the tyre, I knew that there was a tyre depot just down the road and it was open on a Sunday.

The tyre shop would be the first port of call, I told the receptionist my problem, he agreed to check for us and repair as necessary, he did find a screw lodged in the rear tread but it had not had chance to work through the tyre carcase, he removed it. He charged me £10.00, we were all were happy with the outcome, once more we were on our way.

Dropping Suzy off, she gave me a big hug and the wettest kiss I have ever had, she alighted from the vehicle, when she got to the door, and safely inside she looked back at me blowing a kiss, then slipping down her dress, she shook her breasts at me, now thinking to myself, I would like to see those boys again.

Contented I drove back to the yard.

Chapter 21

The yard gate was open when I got back, Les was dropping off a car from the small tow truck. The front end of the car had taken a serious impact and the driver's side door pillar had squashed down a bit, scratch marks were across the roof of the car, lumps of earth and grass were sticking out from sections of the car.

"What happened here?" I asked It was on the bypass this chap had a blow out and he went down the embankment and turned it over. The driver is in hospital and he is poorly, also he had dried blood on his shirt, a large sticky plaster on his face, it looked as if he had been in an accident before. and they found your business card in his top pocket. He passed me the card Yes it was the card I had given to Matt earlier this morning.

Shove this car on the lift I want to look, I gave this man first aid this morning and he was on his way home, he was ok then. I am going to get changed. Rushing into the flat I changed in double quick time, this time making sure my pants were up before I set off, down to the workshop, Les already had the car on the lift, raising it up to head height, what are we looking for, nails or screws in the tyres or just about anything to make this car crash. "We found three screws and what may have been a cut in the front flexible brake pipe, this is on the accident side, Les suggested. but it, could have been cut in the crash.

"Those screws I bet I have some as well."

"Where from"?

"The dance we were at last night".

"How, why, what for"?
"I don't know". I fetched the collection of screws from the Motorhome and compared the screws, an exact match. Now who else has screws in their tyres it is important that all who attended have their tyres checked and quickly.

A police Accident investigation unit, drove into the yard and parked up. As the officer approached me,
I remarked "have you ever heard the term in the right place at the right time"?
"Yes" the officer said
"You have come to see"?
"The car you have on the lift",
"I thought so" I wanted to know what the police knew before I put my idea's forward. I talked with one of the offices as the other started taking details from the car, making a tea always helps.
Telling him about the bashing the driver got at the Saturday evening dinner dance, and then how he woke me up this morning.
Suzy cleaned him up and gave him some tea,
He said he was off home as his wife would think he had another woman.
Then the last I saw was him driving off down the road, his name was Matt, I didn't know his last name. That is correct a Mr Matt Simmons,
I know them now, Simmons's Haulage, Pink, and Cream wagons our fathers were best of mates but I didn't know his son.
But if that was his son, I do know him now. Tea made we carried cups out to the inspection area. The other

inspector could not find anything else that could have caused the accident. I showed him the screws that I found under the Motorhome and the cut to the brake hose, He replied that screws can come from anywhere, yes, and both our vehicles where at the same car park last night, then I thought of something asking Les to bring and put the motorhome on the other lift; I wanted to check something out. Lifting the mobile home, I looked for cuts in the brake hose, sure enough there was a similar cut in the brake hose. Even for me that is too much of a coincident, the officer asked to remove the brake pipes and they would like to have the cuts analysed at the police forensic labs, before we started to dismantle, he photographed all the interesting points. I locked the motorhome brakes off, and removed the cut pipe, Les removing the one from the crashed car, the officer labelled them, and placed each hose and the screws in sample bags. the officer asked "Who have you upset. "Not me I never said a word", it was DS Harper. "What has he to do with this, he is working on a suspect culprit at the moment and I reckon he would appreciate a call on the incident." Les had fitted a new brake hose to the motorhome while I was talking with the officer. He was happy with what he had and would be checking in with us in a few days. Somebody does not like us Les, we are being targeted.

Chapter 22

As I looked around the bottom of the motorhome, there was a place for another fuel tank, the area was dust free, and something had sat there but it isn't now, I wonder where that went to, we haven't removed anything, and the only guy that removed anything was John Wade.

He claimed he had drained the tank, or could he have taken one off and put another back on.

If so, why?

He said, it was contaminated, what with?

John Wade said, he found a pair of knickers floating around in the tank, and a plastic bag what other plastic bags, or what was in water proof plastic, diesel proof plastic bags.

Looking at the floor above where the tank fitted the motorhome floor, tapping it over the area and a small amount of road dust fell and revealed a mark on the floor, giving it a bigger knock more road dust fell away.

There was a gap, Les brought over an airline and he fitted a long-nosed air blasting, nozzle. Then the dust in that crevice was eradicated.

Following the joint line, he discovered a square, a hatch, I clambered inside the motorhome, then found approx. where the square was, it was underneath the small vertical cupboard calling out to Les to blast some air up the joint to see where it comes through the floor.

Les blowing air I was holding my hand but I could not feel any air coming into the cabin.

Lifting the carpet Les tried again, no air flowing, lifting the vinyl flooring a small round hole the size of a petrol cap was there, try again I found something still no air was being felt. Les got an inspection lamp and held it close to the floor, any light shining through, nope nothing, I tried pressing the circle it was solid, I tried to turn it, no purchase for my finger to get hold of it, "Shall we drill the floor".

"Why not, let's find out what this panel is hiding", Drilling a hole, Les pushed in a welding rod it has a depth of 40 mm Anything dripping or falling out of the hole? "Nope,"

Where is that probe camera Kevin has, in his toolbox the large yellow one in the corner, Les drills a small hole so we Inserted the probe, watching the viewing screen we could now see into the panel looking around nothing just an empty space.

but then, something at the far end pushing the probe deeper a bundle of papers, pulling the probe back and pushing it the opposite direction a couple of envelopes like what we got from the wall lining.

Pulling the camera probe backwards slowly, I saw an electrical wire, coloured brown, and grey matching the wood finish, I almost missed it.

Looking where it went to, it disappeared through the panel into the bulkhead, going back to the other end of the wire it enters an electrical connector block just near the centre of the floor.

I just thought of something, walking back to the work bench I picked up a heavy duty magnetic, I thought, I would search for the metal catch using the magnet. Moving the magnet over the underneath the floor it wasn't finding anything to adhere to.

Just Three Lads

Les scratching his head this is a beauty how do you get in with destroying anything, it must be simple, if is used as a secret compartment, must have a hidden access point, even if it took a day to open it and close it.

If investigating officers could not find it, it had worked. Where was John Wade looking when we found him, going back to the area Les blasted the dirt off nothing but a nut head sticking through the chassis, but on the other side the bolt did not protrude through, placing a socket wrench on the nut it turned, reasonable stiffly then an audible click was heard, even from three feet away.

Les said, "Bro" it has moved.

"What moved" The floor, he was hanging onto it to stop it springing back. Trying to pull it down it wouldn't budge, Les pulled the shelf and moved the nut with the spanner again, that was it the panel slid towards him, another hinge came into play, causing the panel to swing downwards on side brackets, thus giving access to the secret compartment.

Les shone his light in the compartment then could see the bundle of papers, pulled them out of the hidden section, shining his lamp in the compartment nothing else was found, then turning the lamp the other direction, we pulled out thirty or more envelopes they just kept coming the compartment ran nearly the full length of the motorhome. Finally, the compartment was clear. boy was I happy with that, looking on the other side of the vehicle, to see if there was a compartment as well the floor plan was a different shape, with the exhaust layout into where a cavity could have been placed.

Just Three Lads

The pile of envelopes, I placed into a large cardboard box, and took them into the office, there was no room in the safe for this lot. where could I put them safe for a while. Kevin's bedroom nobody goes there, then again nobody used to go to my bedroom, Les's bedroom currently was like Waterloo station.

Then I thought of something crazy, getting a black marking pen from the office I wrote on the side of the box and pushed it up on top of the metal filing cabinet in my office.

Les came into the office "Aha you have hidden what we found.

The floor is back in place once you pushed it back it just slips into place, cover it with the tank and road dust, it wouldn't be found in a hurry.

I put the interior back as well.

"Oops" Les said "What about this bundle of papers; I forgot to put them in the box, he dropped them on to my desk". asking "What do I do with these?

"Well, the most obvious is why not read them, and see if we find out exactly who, is after us, and what for"?

An impressively well-endowed young lady, entered the office, "Hello Les, I am here, are you ready"?

"My afternoon meeting" he replied with a glint in his eye. "Ok have fun, you will have to tell me where you find such women" I said and they walked off toward his flat.

Chapter 23

Closing the garage, I brought the bundle of papers with me to my flat, made myself a coffee sat down and started to read.

Documents for disposal was written across the front of the folders.

The first folder just had case number 408js on the front page, Jimmy, and Suzy' plus their surname was written in pencil. I read the entire file, at the end of the file a number, some letters, like a filing system. No numerical figures were shown in the file just what actions had happened, and whether payment had been received or not. I started on the second file, A widow lady, hers was distressing story of losing a husband to cancer, and lost out on the compensation claim because of some trivial problem, yet payment seems to have been received. Another file with similar cases all dealing with claims and payments received and huge payments deducted for the legal work. At the end of what had seen and read their story was the same. Wondering what Suzy's first actual document said and what she finally was paid. I called her and said what I had found. She would be very interested in seeing the file as well as seeing me, I said "I would bring it round this afternoon and compare". The box where the other letters were stored, I pulled down from the cabinet, placing the other documents in, and then removing one of the sealed envelopes a number like the number on the file was written on the bottom corner. Searching through the envelopes, I found the matching numbers. Closing the yard, I took both envelopes round to Suzy's house. She was glad to see me and gave me a big hug, and a lingering kiss, the girls were doing their homework quietly on the table.

Suzy had the initial document that she was given and, comparing the pages in the file the page was the last one was taken from the actual file.

She received Three Thousand Two Hundred and Fifty pounds. She should have Three Hundred and Twenty-Five Thousand pounds. Now opening the last envelope, tipping the bundles of bank notes on the floor, let us count this lot and see what we have. The girls spied the bundle of money; immediately stopped their homework and rushed to helped count the money.

Asking was this theirs could they have this and that. I insisted that we need to know what we have, they could think it was a hands-on maths lesson.

The eldest girl retrieved pen and paper from the table and proceeded to make a list of the bundles and then the quantity of the notes in each bundle, and giving total at the end. The sum of money came too. Actual cash 321 packets of £1000 = £321,000.00 1 packet of £750.00 =£ 750.00 A cheque for = £ 3, 250.00 Total = £325, 000.00. Letting Suzy see the file reference number, and the money bag reference numbers, they matched.

This is yours, what you were expecting to receive, and in conclusion this is what you should have received from the Sangster crew.

"What a bunch of bloody crooks" Suzy swore vigorously.

Now may I suggest that you either hide this money or we get into a safe place?

Just Three Lads

As we chatted, we packed the packets of notes back into the envelope. "Where can you suggest"?
"Well, if you book into a hotel in the town, you could put the envelope in their safe",
"I don't trust anyone, walls have ears".
A little laugh came back from the youngest girl, "Now you are being silly walls don't have ears, do they"?
Or it can go into the office safe and you bank it tomorrow. also, nobody knows what you have here, so in a way it is safe or you could sleep on it.
Suzy looked at me and mouthed "We sleep on it and we could make love on it"
My eyes widened with the offer and I whispered "That would be nice."
The eldest girl looked at her mum then whispered "If you want to go and make love that is ok, we don't mind, after all we are grown up now"
"I looked at Suzy with me being aware my mouth was open, Suzy stood up closed my mouth with her finger then took my hand.
Follow me Mr. we went to bed for the rest of the afternoon.
I stayed the night at Suzy's the girls were accepting me as mum's new bloke, and just got on with life.
Suzy and I chatted in bed about what we were going to do with the rest of the money.
It is not ours and it belongs to the clients who were swindled. We could cross reference, the files with money bags, maybe let the Police handle the giving of the cash back to customers.
Then it would keep us out of it totally.

Chapter 24

My phone rang it was Les, we have been turned over, the safe has been broken into and the office is a mess,
"Ok we, will be down in a few minutes", Shit, bugger, all that money, and left in an open box on top of a filing cabinet. Bugger, my name will be a laughing stock for ages. Quickly we drove back to the office, Les and two patrol officers and another forensic officer, were looking for fingerprints, also taking doing their stuff, taking notes, photographs, and dusting for finger prints.
DS Harper had just arrived on another matter,
Oh, dear whenever I come, the rest of the police force is here as well, you could open a social club here?
It would be easier to get here than the Police station.

One of the patrol guys stated "I think that this will be an easy case;" forensics took our finger prints, the officer checked out our prints against what they had found; he was disappointed no new ones were found.
A plastic piece of pipe hung from the diesel tank gave an indication someone had been siphoning the diesel as well.
The forensic officer called out to Les who was just about to pull the siphon tube out.
"Don't touch it he said, I have a theory" he pulled out some cotton swabs and took a sample from the end of the pipe where the thief must have sucked on to get the diesel flowing.
"What will that prove"? Les enquired "DNA" was the reply. The office was blitzed the safe was a mess but

they still had not managed to get the door open the petty cash tin had gone from Suzy's desk, and her files were strewn all over.

Poor Suzy was crying "It is my entire fault."

If I hadn't come to work here you wouldn't have been targeted.

DS Harper looked at me and raised an eyebrow can you elaborate on her statement.

My gaze switched from DS Harper, to where the box was, phew I sighed, it was still there and it looked unbelievably untouched.

What is special about a box marked MT envelopes & tax returns written on it? DS Harper enquired. "Bullshit baffles brains".

"Well yesterday Les and I decided to find out what we could find in the motorhome, since I had been driving it around it has attracted so much attention, I told DS H, the history so far. It had been attacked at the dinner dance and the brake lines cut".

"We found that it used to have two fuel tanks fitted; I have a mind to think it still had the twin tanks fitted, when it broke down and I took it to John Wade's garage. The same time that Suzy had to go to Sangster's for her insurance claim payment".

"Still with me"?

"Yes"

"Now if John Wade didn't have enough time to remove the fuel tank and empty the secret compartment, as I returned early, he had only removed the second fuel tank which I had filled from my fuel bowser in my yard.

he simply sealed off the second fuel pipe and as the main tank was empty, I had to refill with diesel at his place.
Ok but he charged me two hundred pounds for his Diesel.

He said that my fuel was contaminated, and then gave me back a pair of lady's knickers, claiming he found in the tank and a plastic bag, whether they came from inside the tank I don't know.

But I bet the second tank is at John Wade's garage and full of my diesel.
Now I drove it back without a problem, so it may have been the diesel, it may not, no matter, it could have been the knickers bunging up the pickup pipe or the plastic bag doing that as well who knows.

Later John Wade came here and broke into the yard the same evening, and tried to break into the van from underneath, he only had two pry-bars and one wrench with him. Going to my desk and retrieving two pry bars and a 15mm wrench, the same size as the special nut on the chassis that when you turn it one way part of the floor drops down to give you access to the secret compartment.

Now we have found that when we got into it, there were lots of paper envelopes that contain thousands of pounds. and some office files, like what you already have from the car with the smashed in back end.
"Affirmative" DS Harper murmured.

One of these files had Suzy and Jimmy's name on its Jim being Suzy's deceased husband, who was killed in that Motorhome. Then I went on to explained how I had worked that out.

The officers both nodding in agreement.

Suzy's mouth had fallen open, "Close your mouth darling" I said looking at her; her mouth closed I continued.

Now in all the problems I have sorted out I still can't explain the ladies' knickers in the van or the box of sex toys we found in the draw.

Les holding up a finger, "Bro I may be able to help you, these probably belong to some of my ladies they seem recently to have a habit of coming to see me not wearing them". So, where they dispose of them was a mystery until now.

"The toys? one girl did bring some and when we used the motorhome a few times they may have been left in there". DS Harper, "Interesting explanation, and I cannot argue with that statement."

"The only other thing is the gold ring that I found it isn't mine and it is a small fitting, it was in my top draw of my desk pulling out the draw it had gone, it had engraved "From me to You" inside the ring.

Suzy sat down with a thump her mouth opens again.

"Ok tell us that it is yours",

"No, it was Jim's, I gave it to him a few weeks for his birthday and had it engraved by the jeweller in the town".

The mention of gold made me think about the gold cufflink I found in the car park, retrieving it from my suit pocket I passed it to DS Harper.

"This I found in the car park next to the guy called Matt Simson, who had been attacked, it may have come from the attacker"?

"Thanks for that" then he made a note in his book then proceeded to asked me

"How did you work out the connection"?

"Each file was marked for destruction and the money envelopes or bags, had corresponding file numbers written on them".

"Suzy had a file with and number on it and she also had the document she should have signed, to release her final payment.

She had left it on my desk, I read it yesterday and saw the number, and previously I had noticed numbers on the money envelopes".

"Cross checking the numbers I matched file and money envelope,

I then took them round to Suzy let her open the paperwork and check out what I have found, her daughters counted the money and low and behold the cash amount was correct in the envelope".

"There were a few more files, I have them in the car and I will let you see them, after Charles my solicitor, who should be arriving soon gives them the once over".

"But in that box are all the money files"? asked the one of the officers.

Replying, this is something I don't know, how long this fraud or racket has gone on, but if all the reckoning is correct what has been going on in that office can be backward estimated by interviewing previous clients.

That is a job for you guys.

"Harper asked, why did I not put them in the safe"?

"I was under pressure to put the files somewhere all our lock-ups are full, so I wrote empty MT Envelopes and old tax returns on the box, if anyone looked inside, it was files and envelopes. What it says on the box is not always what is inside.

Anything else may have been pulled down and opened".

Just on cue Charles breezed in through the door.

He quickly grasped the situation browsing through what we had found.

"This is the key to the whole scam these guys have been working".

"We may not get them all; but once the story goes to the press there will be further enquiries".

Suzy came to my side, she looked sad, she didn't want to go in the motorhome again, that is where Jimmy died. I couldn't live with that.

Remembering, John Wade wanted to buy the motorhome, well what happens if I say it is for sale.

Anyone who knows what it was used for would, come out of the woodwork.

I sell it to John Wade, I take it to his workshop I sell it, get paid for the vehicle, let him start playing with it, then you guys go and check out the premises, then you will as they say catch him red handed.

DS Harper thought a better idea, also if he has the original diesel tank for that vehicle somewhere on his premises, that is another nail in his coffin. Plus, whatever you guys turn up.

John Wade as he said fell out with Sangster, and would probably do anything to get one on him. So, the motorhome is up for sale, the guide price for this one is £146,000, I will ask a snip of a price of £100,000 for it are you guys ready to go with that, DS Harper called his boss, put the latest plan to him, he was delighted, and ready to go with the operation.

Making a telephone call to the accursed ex-mate John Wade, I said although I did say you could have 1st refusal Ok mate thanks for the offer",

"We have put a price on it of £100 K,"

"Strewth, what do you think it is made of gold plate"? John Wade cried

"No mate it is like money in the bank, these motorhomes are climbing in price.

Anyway, that's it take it or leave it, that old friend of your Sangster may be interested as well".

"You have four hours; I am coming your way later on and could deliver it if you like".

Ok he will get back to me, Normal terms are cash or certified banker's order. He agreed.

"I think it is time for a coffee"; Suzy quick on the command had washed the cups and making the brew, passed round to the guys, Harper said to Suzy better make another as the Police chief just drove into the yard.

He had heard about the proposed, operation and wanted first hand info,

Harper and the officers got the chief up to speed, Charles told him on the legal side in selling the truck to probably the man, who converted it, and if he had spare parts, for that camper it showed he had more than a commercial interest in the vehicle.

The yard started to get busy, another tow truck arrived to take the crashed bus away, and other transporter for six of the crashed cars, Kevin, and Les working well, started to load the cars onto the car transporter, the yard was emptying quickly.

The wagon with the wire coils, was repaired and that was ready to go, Suzy called the company, they said they can send a driver to bring it away. That just left cars and the container truck, what is the contents DS Harper enquired, I don't know, Kevin, he will know. Alas Kevin never got chance to look inside he just covered the tear in the metal, he grabbed a ladder and went to investigate. Calling from his observation point, he saw two cars inside with boxes sat on top of a wooden frame.

The chief of police requested that we open it and check contents, Kevin's special lock removal tool made short work of the padlocks, the doors swung open to reveal a high-quality sports car than an expensive Range Rover at the far end, the sports car was parked underneath a mezzanine floor with boxes of car parts stacked up on top plus engines gearboxes and rear axles.

Any chance of getting inside and reading out the serial numbers, the police chief asked, Kev tried he was too bulky, one of the offices removed his body armour and managed to squeeze in, called out what numbers he could see.

DS Harper checked on his laptop, he remarked funny how both cars were one number shy on the chassis number from registered stolen vehicles.

The office squeezed back out of the container. With this scant information the chief, requested the container be emptied and all parts checked against the stolen parts list.

Suzy dug out the customers details, and behold a name came up that was known to me and the police. This belongs to our mate John Wade.

This is getting better, I added. Is there a destination? Harper placed a call; we will know in a few minutes. "Russia for the cars and spare parts possible for Africa or the middle east market, even the internet auction market."

My mobile rang, it was John Wade he has managed to get the money together and would have cash for me about mid-afternoon,

"Ok I will see you then".

The chief went back to his office to coordinate with the chief of police at the town, we were going to visit,

Harper said that he would accompany me so there was two he would follow me in the car, so it looked correct to John Wade two cars in and one to go back.

Harper said what car can we use, asking Kevin is your car ready for the road, and can I borrow it, for a couple of hours today, no problem, Bro it is ready to go.

The driver from the haulage came to remove the wagon with the steel coils, the load had moved and the driver had to pretension the entire load again with chains and clamps adding a couple more for extra security.

Just Three Lads

He was trying to nose around the container, but was moved on by one of the police officer's,
He pulled out of the yard and went on his way, now just Sangster's flatbed truck and the container remained in the yard and a couple of cars.
Cleaning out the motorhome of personal items that we had left in it, Harper and I prepared to start our final trip to John Wade's garage,
I was now equipped with a radio wire to have my conversation recorded.
Two hours later I pulled the motorhome and car onto John Wade's forecourt, his garage had two floors above and a lift to take cars to the different floor levels; it was an impressive building, an old design but a purpose made garage from the 1950.
John Wade was in the showroom watching as we pulled in, asking how was the drive in Kevin's car? fast and it handles good, I am impressed.

We were laughing about it as we walked into the showroom, "What's the joke"? John Wade enquired, we told him about borrowing Kevin's car, and old Harper, thinks it is brilliant.
I get to drive it back.
"Ok here are the documents for the motorhome and the transfer document is signed".
John Wade returned and passed me an envelope and I opened the it and counted out 100, sealed packets of £1000, stamped and sealed from the bank, I rechecked the amount of cash bundles, 99 your one bundle shy,
John Wade grumbled and pulled open a draw and produced the final packet.

Just Three Lads

Oh, there it is it must have fallen back into the draw.

"Ok Yeah but deal done, I passed him the keys and electronic key fob, I can't get the key fob to work it probably needs a battery, I won't shake your hand, see you sometime".

Then Harper and I walked out and got into Kev's car, and slowly drove out of the garage, across the road turned the corner, and parked up.

We went for a coffee in the happy burger bar across the road from John Wade's garage.

then watched and waited. Within ten minutes a black car swung into the garage and drove round to the back workshop. then three suited figures walked in the showroom, it was Sangster, with the steroid twins, they approached John Wade took the keys from him and it was either Dum, or Dee, walked out and got into the motorhome, and cautiously, drove it towards the rear of the garage and unfortunately, we lost sight of it.

We were munching on a good cheeseburger and fries when we were joined by another chap dressed in a tee shirt jeans and trainers; he flashed his badge and said everything was ready to roll.

Suggesting that Harper and myself, sit and watch from here as everyone in the squad knows each other and new faces may cause a problem.

but we can come and see later after they have sorted out what they were going to do.

A coach full of a rugby team pulled onto the forecourt and parked near the diesel pump, the guys got out and tried to push the bus towards the pump. bus wasn't moving, the driver was shouting at them to push harder, the banter from the guys was heard inside the burger bar.

John Wade and a mechanic came out to help, he looked underneath and when they walked round the blind side of the bus two of the rugby guys grabbed them both opening a side door, John Wade, and the mechanic, were bundled inside.

The rest of the guys still joking on trying to push the bus gave up, one said he was going to use the bathroom to take a pee, two of them walked round the back to see where the toilet was, Twiddle Dum came back out with one guy, pointing to a door where the bathroom was; one guy talking to Dum while one went to the toilet.

They were laughing about something, when suddenly the guy offered to shake Dum's hand, then quickly swung him round, and hand cuffed his hands so quick. Dum shouted the warning and all the squad of special branch guys ran into the garage.

Harper and I were now outside on the pavement watching, then a scream of tyres and the black car shot out of the garage driving across the forecourt smashing through a low wall and sped off down the road by the side of us. Harper said let's go and follow him see where he goes, jumping into Kevin's car we took off in the direction of the black car, Harper's police radio crackled they had Twiddle Dee and Dum in custody, so that leaves Sangster in the car on his own, we saw the car in front and we were gaining on it, DS Harper said drop back a bit, we can't really stop it let the patrol guys do it. Harper said where about we were on the trunk road; they are setting up a road block further down the road. Still gaining on the black car, we saw the road block, and the black car wasn't slowing, he tried to make through the gap, left between the police cars, clipped one car, the impact of the collision caused the black car to weave and spin out of control, rolling onto its driver's side as it slid down the ditch. The cars boot lid had sprung open and boxes of paperwork had fallen out of the car, looking they were more files for disposal, In the corner of the boot a box of wood screws identical to the ones we found in the car park, pointing these items out to DS Harper. I climbed up onto the side of the car I opened the door looking into the interior chasm two people were struggling to get out. I offered my hand to the first hand reaching out and then pulled up a person I didn't really like, firmly but surely, I lifted him out of the car and let him get his foot hold on the grass embankment, then reaching down into the chasm again I lifted the other passenger she was much lighter to lift, she clung onto my arm as I lifted and I let her down next to her companion. Swiftly looking inside, I spotted what looked like a shotgun poking out from under the rear seat squab, that had moved when the car turned onto its side. There were no more occupants, I let the door close, jumped down then it was my turn standing on the embankment. "Hello Mr Sangster and Hello Lizzy, "Would you like me to call a tow truck, "Your vehicle is quite damaged. then a strange event happened, Sangster made a run at me, what to do, I am not sure, but, remembering what Farmer Ian had once said, about dumb beasts, making a show of who is master by charging, the trick Ian had worked out, I stepped back, raised my hand gesturing for him to stop, Ian had formed his hand into a fist. I was caught unawares and held my hand out as warning to Halt. Sangster heeded no such gesture, and then collided with my open palm, my fingers poked him in the eyes, and the base of my palm connecting with his chin.

That was a bad move mate, my arm was straight I was standing as if I was ready to stop a runaway horse, the resounding click I heard was his teeth as they connected, his head stopped moving but his body didn't, legs up to elbow level and down he went, Landing into a wet area of mud and tyre marks, he just lay there not moving, I didn't move anticipating another attack. he was down and he was out. Bravo, Lizzy cried, I have been waiting to see something like that happen to him for ages, the Traffic officers ran up and turned him over on the ground and putting hand cuffs on him, I remarked that he has now a muddy suit matching on both sides.

As they took Lizzy away, she looked at me, remarking, keep in touch, we did have a good time once. replying politely, I said, I do not think I would like too again.

Later in the day I was back at the garage, Harper had called to say, Twiddle Dum had in his pocket Suzy's ring, Twiddle Dee when arrested was pressing the key fob like a mad man at the motorhome, one of our technicians took a close inspection and found that the key fob was connected to an empty box built into the motorhome, we reckon if a charge had been laid in there it would have destroyed any evidence within. he had the other half of the gold cuff link in his pocket, it matched the one I had found.

Also, the technician told me later he had found that wire to the explosive charge which was missing, making a mental note to myself to tell Kevin the wrapped-up item he has under his bed is a bomb.

I would do that when I got back. Strange how none of them owned up to owning the shotgun found in the car, later in the month, the headlines in the newspaper that a Local Law Firm was under police investigation for a £500 million fraud, It would appear that the group had been involved in the diverting of funds from clients account to their bank in Lichtenstein, Jimmy had evidently worked out what they were doing and when they found the 50k on him they assumed he was taking money from the packets, Lizzy was the undercover spotter spy, sleeping with all and sundry making sure she got her cut, when a DNA test was done on her. Her finger prints and DNA matched what was found in the motorhome after the crash, she admitted being involved in the crash to stop Jimmy going to the police, and she considered herself equal to Sangster and was making her own career without care for who she hurt on the way.

Many clients where refunded the money they were owed and the company of solicitor's were struck from the legal profession, Charles was doing well, after the case ended, and he brought his car in for new brake discs and brake pads to be fitted them then as luck has it, we pulled in the same model car but younger and a very low mileage, it was in perfect condition. We swapped the car to him for his pending bill, saying we would include all the services that he may require in with the deal. We had been rewarded a substantial contract from the Insurance companies and an acceptable reward for the discovery of information leading to a huge fraud being discovered. Kevin was on holiday with somebody, Les was now reasonably well known and his pick of the ladies was increasing. Suzy had received all her funds back, also

after her six weeks trial period, decided to stay on and make tea and coffee, supplying the Carrot cake now and again, funny how on those days we have lots of visitors. Then a day or two later I was reliably informed that the new president of the Road Haulage Association had been voted off the control board. Suzy did later confide in me that she remembered me describing her Mum, in my dream, when we were laying on the bed, her Mum had also died in an accident a year previous and she and Jimmy were great friends. At the time she didn't know what I was going to say about her and this started to freak her out, so she just feigned fainting, but the collision of our heads had made her see stars and dazed she really felt sick., I did not reply to Suzy about what she said often mulling the conversation in my mind. A couple of days
 turned into a couple of weeks business had become very quiet; mentioning to Suzy. It's very quiet, strange how nothing exciting is happening. Do you often feign actions in what you do?
Suzy looked at me, her facial expression changed to a mischievous smile.
Come with me Mr, I will show you real and fake.

Is this, THE END.

Oh, No Mr, there is going to be a tomorrow.

THE END or THE END.
Whatever end is your preference

PS, Kevin was informed about his dangerous new found package, laid under his bed, he removed it to the middle of the yard, he was disappointed he expected a big loud bang, but instead it smouldered and caught fire.

Printed by Amazon Italia Logistica S.r.l.
Torrazza Piemonte (TO), Italy

41665670R00136